DOCTOR WHO

Paradox Lost

The DOCTOR WHO series from BBC Books

Paradox Lost

GEORGE MANN

BOOKS

1 3 5 7 9 10 8 6 4 2

Published in 2011 by BBC Books, an imprint of Ebury Publishing.
A Random House Group Company

Doctor Who is a BBC Wales production for BBC One.
Executive producers: Steven Moffat, Piers Wenger and Beth Willis

The Random House Group Limited Reg. No. 954009

Addresses for companies within the Random House Group can be found at
www.randomhouse.co.uk

A CIP catalogue record for this book is available from the British Library.

ISBN 978 1 849 90235 9

The Random House Group Limited supports the Forest Stewardship
Council® (FSC®), the leading international forest certification
organisation. All our titles that are printed on Greenpeace approved
FSC® certified paper carry the FSC® logo. Our paper procurement
policy can be found at www.randomhouse.co.uk/environment

Commissioning editor: Albert DePetrillo
Editorial manager: Nicholas Payne
Series consultant: Justin Richards
Project editor: Steve Tribe
Cover design: Lee Binding © Woodlands Books Ltd, 2011
Production: Rebecca Jones

Printed and bound in Great Britain by Clays Ltd, St Ives PLC

To buy books by your favourite authors and register for offers,
visit www.randomhouse.co.uk

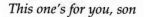

This one's for you, son

London, 13 October 1910

He'd never intended to become a thief.

Edgar Miller considered this as he wedged the end of his crowbar against the sill and began to prise open the sash window. He'd always planned to do something worthwhile with his life, to make something of himself. Life, however, had pointedly refused to provide him with any opportunities. For years he'd tried to earn an honest living, breaking his back with manual work, mucking out stables, fetching and carrying. In the end, though, where had that gotten him? He'd been forced to slog his guts out while watching others sit back and grow fat on the fruits of his labour. In the end it had simply proved too much, and a month earlier he had finally taken matters into his own hands. There were easier ways to put food on the table.

The sash window gave way with a noisy splinter of wood, and Miller paused for a moment, listening for any sign that someone might have heard. The night was silent save for the sounds of a tabby cat prowling about in the flowerbeds and the distant clatter of horse's hooves. He gently placed the crowbar on the ground and slid the window up in its frame, wincing as the mechanism creaked loudly in protest.

Miller swung himself in through the window and dropped softly to the kitchen floor on the other side. The room was cast in long shadows, illuminated only by the thin sliver of moonlight that slanted in through the still-open window. He could see shapes hulking in the gloaming: a table, a dresser, a stove. None of these were likely to yield the sort of prizes he was searching for.

Miller crept towards the door, stopping to listen for sounds of movement from deeper within the old house. He smiled to himself as he reached for the door handle. The place might as well have been deserted. If he was lucky, he'd be out of there in a matter of minutes, his pockets stuffed full of baubles he could fence down at the Rose and Crown the following day.

The hallway beyond the door was long and narrow, but filled with all manner of ostentatious decoration: a gilt-framed mirror, a tall vase brimming with peacock feathers, a telephone table proudly displaying the latest receiver. Again, he continued on his way, determined that the stuff of real value would be found elsewhere in the house.

The dining room proved immediately more fruitful, and within a few moments Miller had already relieved the sideboard of its silver cutlery service, shovelling it into a cloth sack he'd brought with him for the purpose.

He started at a sudden sound from upstairs, pausing with a silver ashtray in his hand. His breath came in ragged gasps. What had it been? The mewling of an animal? A family pet? He remembered he'd seen the tabby cat in the backyard. Yes, that must have been it. The cat had probably followed him in through the open window. Nothing to worry about. Cautiously, he continued with his work.

Miller wondered if the family was at home. The mistress of the house would surely have a well-appointed jewellery box, and a treasure trove such as that would mean he wouldn't have to do another job for weeks, if not longer. He decided it was worth the risk to find out.

He left the sack of cutlery at the bottom of the stairs as he crept up towards the bedrooms, his footfalls accompanied by the ominous ticking of the grandfather clock in the hall below. Every sound seemed magnified, echoing out around the still and silent house. If he found someone asleep in the master bedroom, well, he would turn about and hotfoot it out of there the same way he had come, collecting the sack on the way.

The floorboards on the landing groaned as he presented them with his weight, and he found himself tiptoeing along, his back pressed to the wall. His breath was coming in short, ragged gasps. Sweat was prickling on his forehead. Until now, he'd confined himself to quick, relatively minor incursions into people's homes, but now he was taking a real risk. If something happened, if he was caught… well, it would mean the cells, or worse. For a moment he considered turning back. The silver service was enough, surely? He could sense the danger. Yet something made him go on. Whether it was the promise of the treasures he might find, or simply the adrenalin that was pounding through his veins, he had no idea.

Miller passed the door to the guest room, stopping only momentarily to peer inside. It was difficult to see anything in the gloom, but the bed appeared to be made. He considered heading inside to poke around in the drawers, but decided to press on to the master bedroom instead. Anything else was just an unnecessary delay.

Further along the landing, the door to the master bedroom stood ajar. Miller loitered on the threshold for a few moments, attempting to gather himself. He would step in, he decided, take stock, and then back out onto the landing while he decided what to do. If the coast was clear, he would locate the jewellery box and scarper.

Careful to make as little sound as possible, Miller crept into the room. In here, the curtains had been pulled shut against the moonlight and it took a moment for his eyes to adjust to the darkness. When they did, Miller immediately found himself wishing they had not.

The two people in the bed – a husband and wife, he presumed – lay still on their backs beside each other, both staring up at the ceiling. Their faces were fixed in expressions of appalled horror, and dark blood trickled from their unseeing eyes, pooling on the pillows beneath them. It was one of the most horrific sights that Miller had ever seen. He felt his chest tighten in panic and fear. But it was the sight of the creature looming over the two corpses that caused Miller's knees to almost buckle in terror.

The thing was like something derived from a nightmare, a creature dragged from the very depths of Hell. It was humanoid and stood on its hind legs, but its body was strangely angular, as if its pallid grey flesh had been stretched too taut over its bones. Beneath its arms fleshy membranes hung loose, and its face was hideous, with an upturned snout and a mouth glistening with needle-sharp teeth. Its body appeared to be smooth and entirely hairless, and its eyes flashed red in the gloom.

The creature turned and bared its fangs, reaching out for Miller with its bony fingers. He stood for a moment, paralysed with fear, as the thing circled the bed, stalking towards him, its clawed fingers twitching with anticipation. He could hear its rasping breath and the click of its talons against the polished floorboards as it came closer, intent, he guessed, on doing to him whatever it had done to the two blood-soaked victims on the bed.

Miller came to his senses. He had to get out of there as quickly as possible. He stepped back, keeping his eyes fixed on the creature, and immediately collided with something behind him. He cried out in panic, fearing it was another of the things come out of the shadows to grab at him, but it was only the door, hanging open where he'd left it.

Steeling himself, Miller spun around and threw himself out of the opening.

The creature issued a horrifying screech – a shrill, piercing scream that seemed to reverberate through his very bones. Then he was out on the landing, hurtling towards the stairs, all sense of caution now gone. He practically threw himself down the staircase, taking the steps three at a time, and didn't look back until he'd made it to the hallway below. A quick glance over his shoulder told him the creature was in fast pursuit.

It was then that his foot caught the edge of the sack he had abandoned in the hallway earlier, sending a couple of knives and forks skittering across the tiled floor. Miller glanced down, weighing up his options. Would it slow him down? He didn't have time to worry about that. He reached down and snatched up the sack, hefting it over his shoulder. Then, turning towards the kitchen, he charged along the hallway, intent on making it out of the window before the thing from upstairs had a chance to catch up with him.

He shouldered his way through the half-open door to the kitchen, slung the sack around as if readying himself to hurl it through the open window, and, too late, realised there were another three of the creatures lurking by the dresser, waiting in the shadows for their prey.

Miller screamed and tried to run, but the creature from upstairs was behind him, and it grabbed at him with its bony fingers, scrabbling for purchase, its talons raking his flesh. It shoved him back toward the others and he fell to his knees, whimpering, before them. 'Wh-what are you?' he managed to stutter.

'We. Are. Squall,' they said, each of them hissing a word in turn. 'And. We. Shall. Feast.'

Miller screamed once again as they descended, and bright blood began to bubble out of his eyes.

Chapter

1

London, 10 June 2789

'Hold on!'

'I *am* holding on!'

'Well… hold on a little tighter, then!' The Doctor shouted this while clutching the TARDIS console and hammering at the controls in what, to Rory, appeared to be a random fashion.

'*Doctor…*' Amy warned.

'Erm… I think you might want to tell her what's going on now, Doctor,' said Rory, in what he hoped was a conciliatory – and not at all panicked – fashion. 'And while we're on the subject, I'd quite like to have a better idea of that myself, too…' He grabbed for the railing and held on for dear life while the entire ship shook and bucked around him. 'I mean, for instance, are we all about to plummet to our deaths, or is this fairly typical for a journey to the Rambalian Cluster?'

The Doctor glanced up from the console, brushing his floppy hair out of his eyes. Rory noticed that, somewhere along the line, the Doctor had discarded his tweed jacket and rolled up his sleeves. His bow tie was slightly off kilter, too. So, serious business, then.

The Doctor met Rory's gaze and offered him an endearing smile. When he spoke again, his tone was calm and measured. 'Well, I… I suppose we're sort of… crashing. In a manner of speaking.' He turned back to the controls, as if that was the end of the matter.

'How can you crash "in a manner of speaking"?' demanded Amy, and Rory could tell the exasperation in her voice was very much affected. In fact, she looked as if she was actually *enjoying* the experience. He, on the other hand, felt decidedly queasy. He'd rather not have been crashing at all, let alone 'in a manner of speaking'.

'Well, not so much *crashing,* as smashing our way through a few roadblocks. Think of it more like a bad case of turbulence,' said the Doctor, nearly tumbling over backwards with a sudden jolt and only managing to maintain his balance by sticking a leg in the air and clinging resolutely to the console. 'The old girl seems to want to take us somewhere in a bit of a hurry and she's jumping a few time tracks in order to do it. Just like a needle skipping in the grooves in an old record.'

Amy looked at him blankly.

'Oh, now I *do* feel old,' he said.

'But why?' Rory asked, his knuckles tightening on the rail as he was nearly knocked from his feet.

'Why do I feel old?' The Doctor asked, with a quizzical expression on his face. 'Well, Rory, it's quite simple, really...'

'Why is the TARDIS taking us somewhere in a hurry?' Amy interjected before the Doctor could continue, rolling her eyes at Rory.

The Doctor beamed. 'That's the bit I haven't worked out yet,' he said, leaning forward to pat the console fondly and glancing up at the time rotor. 'But it's not like you to take shortcuts, is it?'

It took a moment for Rory to realise the Doctor was addressing the ship. As if in response, the TARDIS shuddered and vibrated, and then seemed to settle. Rory watched the Doctor and Amy for a moment as both of them stood back from the console, glanced at each other, and then burst out giggling. Sometimes, he considered, travelling with the Doctor and Amy was like being with two excitable children.

He tentatively let go of the railing, afraid that the ship would suddenly jolt again and he'd go tumbling over the edge of the central platform, but a moment later the TARDIS issued its familiar grating wheeze and landed with a resounding *thump*.

'We're there!' announced the Doctor, rushing around the console, flicking switches and turning dials. He stood back and grasped the sides of the monitor that hung from a bracket attached to the stem of the central column, swinging it around so he could examine the readout.

'Where's "there"?' asked Amy, coming around beside the Doctor, keen not to miss anything. She was wearing a red hoodie, a short black skirt with matching tights, and calf-high black boots. Rory watched her for a minute as she leaned in over the Doctor's shoulder. He still couldn't quite believe that she was his wife. Somehow, he'd managed to marry her, despite everything. He was the luckiest man alive. He went to join them by the console.

'One thing's for sure. It's not the Rambalian Cluster,' the Doctor said, running a hand through his hair. 'Where have you brought us, old girl?' he said quietly, looking suddenly serious. 'And why?' He tapped a fingertip thoughtfully against his forehead and then turned and clapped a hand on Rory's shoulder. 'I suppose there's only one way to find out!' he announced brightly, before leaping down from the central dais and charging toward the door.

Rory watched as the Doctor flung open both doors and disappeared into the bright sunshine that suddenly flooded in from outside. He looked to Amy. She had a mischievous grin on her face. 'We're going after him, then?' he asked.

'Too right we are!' replied Amy, grabbing his hand. 'We're not letting him have all the fun.' She led him down the steps toward the door. The Doctor was waiting for them there, leaning with his back against the doorframe, silhouetted against the bright sun.

'Come along, Pond. Places to go, things to see.'

The Doctor fiddled with his bow tie as if smartening himself up. Rory was surprised to see he'd somehow managed to reclaim his jacket, too. 'And you, Rory. Chop, chop. No time to waste. You're going to want to see this.'

'See what?' said Rory, as he followed the others out into the street. He glanced around, shielding his eyes against the sun and taking in the vista. 'Oh,' he continued. 'That.'

They were standing on the embankment of a wide river, looking out over a futuristic cityscape of the kind Rory had only ever imagined from reading science fiction novels and comic books when he was younger. Glittering towers of metal and glass seemed to extrude from the ground, twisting organically toward the sky. Large, covered complexes sat squat beside the river, built – or perhaps even *grown* – from a substance that resembled pink coral. Huge glass domes encapsulated what looked like forests or plantations amongst all the habitation. Brimming with leafy green trees and lush vines, they punctuated the urban sprawl, little havens of wildlife in the midst of the angular chaos.

Above, the sky was criss-crossed with the vapour trails of scudding aircraft, and below, the river was a hive of activity, buzzing with strange little boats and floating platforms. Amidst all of this shining modernity, however, Rory could see ancient-looking buildings nestling in the shadows, old fashioned brick-built houses and churches of the sort that were old even in his day.

'What is this place?' asked Rory, drinking it all in.

Amy squeezed his hand even more tightly in excitement. 'Is it another alien planet?' she said.

The Doctor shook his head. 'No. It's Earth. London, to be precise. And,' he sniffed at the air, then licked his finger and held it up to the breeze, 'judging by the look and smell of the place, I'd say it was some time in the twenty-eighth century.'

'London?' said Rory, incredulous. 'Really? Everything's so… different.'

The Doctor laughed. 'Am I often wrong about these things, Rory?' Rory shrugged. *Well, you're not always right…* he thought, but kept that particular comment to himself.

'Look, there are the Houses of Parliament.' The Doctor pointed across the river to the now incredibly ancient – but still stately – buildings on the other side. Big Ben remained where it had always stood, proud amongst the surrounding spires that now dwarfed it, but almost lost amongst those later, futuristic developments. 'And that's Westminster Bridge, if I'm not mistaken.' He indicated a little further along the river. 'They manage to preserve a lot of it. At least for another few decades, anyway.'

'What happens in a few decades?'

The Doctor frowned. 'Good question, Rory. But more importantly, why has the TARDIS brought us here, to this specific time and place, and in such a hurry?'

Rory couldn't help thinking the Doctor was

avoiding his question, but nevertheless, he made a good point. They lapsed into silence for a moment while the Doctor seemed to be considering the answer to his own question. He paced back and forth, drumming his fingers against his temples.

'What's going on over there?' asked Amy, who had finally relinquished Rory's hand and had wandered over to the railing that separated the street from the embankment below. She leaned over and pointed to a small group of people who were gathered by the water's edge, lifting something tentatively out of the river on a large pallet. There were at least five men and a woman, plus a handful of divers bobbing up and down in the water, their faces hidden behind breathing apparatus. Large frames of scaffolding had been erected along the embankment close to where they were working, covered in flapping tarpaulins.

The Doctor produced a small pair of binoculars from inside his jacket and put them to his eyes. Not for the first time, Rory wondered where he secreted all of these things, and how he knew what to bring with him. It wasn't as if the Doctor had stopped to raid the equipment cupboard on the way out. Somehow, though, he seemed perpetually prepared for any and all eventualities. 'I don't know, but it looks interesting. Some sort of archaeological dig, from what I can see,' he said, stuffing the binoculars back inside his pocket.

'Then let's go and take a look,' said Amy, starting out in the direction of the excavation. 'You like museums, don't you, Doctor? Here's your chance to see something new.'

'Something old,' Rory corrected her. 'You mean something old.'

Amy seemed to ignore this. After a few steps she turned to look back over her shoulder to see if they were following, and the Doctor caught her eye. 'You've got that look in your eye, Pond.'

'What look?' she replied with mock-sweetness, as if she had no idea at all what he was getting at.

'Like you're planning mischief,' said the Doctor. He grinned at Rory, and then turned back to Amy. 'That's good. I like mischief. Mischief is what we need. Now,' he clapped his hands together with resolve, taking both of them in with an expansive gesture, 'let's go and see what they've found in the river!'

'This looks *spectacularly* interesting,' the Doctor announced loudly and with a little too much enthusiasm, as the three of them walked along the embankment toward the team of archaeologists. A number of the men were huddled around the pallet bickering loudly, preventing Rory from getting a good view of whatever it was they had lifted out of the river. Others were drifting to and fro, ducking in and out of their work tents.

Upon hearing the Doctor's exclamation one of their number, the woman Rory had spotted from above, turned to regard them as they approached. She was clearly in charge: she was holding some sort of complicated computer device for a start, and she was wearing a smart blue suit rather than the more casual attire of the others in her group. She was in her mid-to-late forties, Rory guessed, and was pretty and well coiffured. 'Can I help you?' she said to the Doctor, who raised an eyebrow at her unnecessarily severe tone. He reached for his psychic paper and flashed it before her in a rather cursory fashion.

'I do hope so,' he said. 'We're here to make an inspection.'

The woman narrowed her eyes. 'An inspection, you say?'

The Doctor nodded. 'Yes, that's right. New procedure, nothing to worry about. We just need to take a look at the site to ensure everything is in order.' He loomed over the woman, trying to see, but she blocked his way. 'Everything *is* in order, isn't it?'

'Yes, of course it is,' she said. 'All the finds are being logged and recorded in the marquees over there. I can't imagine there's anything the city conservation board would find interesting, though.'

'City conservation board… right, yes.' The Doctor clicked his fingers. 'Love conservation. So… what's that, on the pallet over there?'

'Nothing but a rusty lump of recently dumped equipment.' She shrugged. 'You'll be wasting your time with that.'

'Nevertheless, we'd still like to take a look.'

'If you must.' The woman stepped to one side to allow the Doctor to pass.

'I'm Amy, by the way,' said Amy, stepping forward and offering the woman her hand. 'This is Rory, and *he's* the Doctor.'

'Hmmm,' said the woman, taking Amy's hand. 'Patricia Young.'

'So what is it you've dredged out of the river, Ms Young?' asked Amy diplomatically, as if in apology for the Doctor. Had they fallen straight into their 'good cop, bad cop' routine, Rory wondered? 'We saw you lifting it out on a pallet,' she went on.

Rory was half listening to the conversation and half trying to see over the Doctor's shoulder as he jostled his way to the front of the assembled group of people and dropped to his haunches, examining the find.

'An Artificial Intelligence unit,' the woman, Patricia, continued. 'It's a recent model, one of those "nearly human" things that have only been on the market for a few months. It's covered in rust and bits of it are missing. Someone's obviously got more money than sense.'

'Why's that?' said Amy.

Patricia gave her a sideways glance. 'Because they cost an absolute *fortune*,' she said, shaking her head. 'More than I could afford. And here's someone dumping one in the Thames.'

'People don't change,' said Rory with a sigh. He turned, glancing up and down the street. He had the vague sense that he was being watched, but he couldn't see anyone else about. He turned back to Patricia and Amy.

Amy gave him an inquisitive look. He shrugged, presuming it was just his imagination. He'd spent so much time with the Doctor of late, he mused, he was beginning to get spooked by his own shadow.

'Amy? Rory? Tell me what you make of this.' The Doctor's voice floated over the noise of the buzzing river tugs. The little cluster of archaeologists had begun to disperse, drifting away to the marquees and – Rory assumed – what they considered to be the more interesting finds.

Rory walked over to stand beside the Doctor. Amy, he realised, was right behind him.

The Doctor was crouched over the pallet, which had been lain out carefully on the embankment and was basically just a plastic stretcher covered in a blue tarpaulin. Upon this makeshift platform rested what looked like the ancient remains of a human being, not unlike a mummy dragged from the bottom of a peat bog. Rory had seen one of those in the British Museum as a child and the image had stayed with him ever since: its twisted, misshapen face, its wrinkled flesh like waxy clay.

This figure was missing one arm and its left leg had gone from below the knee. Its body – a series of interlocking metal plates encasing a steel skeleton, Rory saw as he leaned closer – was thick with brown rust and corrosion. Clumps of rubbery flesh still clung resolutely to its midriff and in patches across its chest. Bunches of exposed wires could be seen between the rusted plates of its joints and its face was frozen in a rictus snarl, enamel teeth exposed in the jaws where the fleshy covering had peeled away.

The Doctor was running his hands over it, a fascinated expression on his face. He reached into his pocket and extracted his sonic screwdriver, flipping it on so that the four fingers of its retractable casing sprung open like petals. He waved it over the AI's head. It emitted its familiar buzzing sound. Then, standing up and spinning around on the spot, the Doctor turned to face Patricia.

'How long did you say these AIs have been on the market?'

Patricia shrugged. 'Two, maybe three months.'

'That's very odd,' said the Doctor, tapping the sonic against his chin. 'Very odd indeed.' He looked across at Amy. 'Because this particular AI has been in the water for centuries.'

Patricia almost guffawed. 'That's impossible!' she said, striding forward. 'Absolutely impossible!'

The Doctor grinned. 'Precisely!' He turned around, clearly animated now. 'But look at it! It's made from a plastic-bonded titanium alloy. State of the art! It could never have corroded like that in a couple of months. It's been in there for ages. And what's more, by lifting it out of the water you've somehow managed to reactivate it. There's some residual power in the chest unit.' He dropped to his knees, once again firing up the sonic. 'If I can just...' he screwed up his face in concentration. 'There!'

One of the AI's eyes suddenly blinked, and Rory took an involuntary step backwards.

'Ow!' shouted Amy, slapping his arm. 'Watch my toes!'

'Sorry,' said Rory sheepishly, shuffling his feet. He found the entire scene rather creepy. It was like watching an ancient corpse suddenly stir and return to life, like something out of a zombie film. Yet he couldn't tear his eyes away from the corroded shell of the AI. He watched with fascination as it tried to turn its head but failed as the rusted joints had little or no movement left in them. Its arm twitched spasmodically, and then it tried to speak.

'Doc… tor…' The word was clear, but spoken in such a broken, mechanical voice that it took Rory a moment to realise its significance. 'Doc… tor…'

'Doctor,' said Amy, putting her hand on his shoulder, the concern evident in her voice. 'It's saying your name.'

'Yes,' he replied. 'Although it's most likely a different person it's asking for. The person who built it, perhaps?'

Rory saw the AI's left eye blink again. There was a dull glow now, emanating from deep within the dark socket. Its head turned fractionally as it tried to look up at the Doctor. 'Doc… tor…'

'Err, Doctor. I actually do think it's you that it wants,' said Rory with a mixture of bafflement and amazement.

'Doc… tor…'

'Yes, I'm here,' said the Doctor. 'I'm here.' He gave the AI another buzz with the sonic. Nothing happened for a second, and then all of a sudden the

AI sat up, twisted to face the Doctor and grabbed the lapel of his tweed jacket in its one remaining fist.

The Doctor started and pulled back, but the AI held him firm, dragging him closer so that his face was near to its own eerie visage. 'Oooh. Interesting,' the Doctor said, with a frown. 'Now I wasn't expecting *that*.'

Rory felt Amy jump behind him. The archaeologists were all backing off, too, Patricia included. 'Doctor...?' Rory said.

The Doctor let out a long exhalation. 'It's all right, Rory. Remain calm. I have the situation *completely* under control.'

The AI shifted slightly in order to glance over at Rory and Amy with its working eye. The sounds of its movements were like the screams of an animal being tortured, as the metal plating, so long in the water, creaked and grated against each other in protest. Rory could hear something else, too, a whirring sound coming from deep inside it. When it turned back to the Doctor it began to speak once more, but this time its voice was calm and measured, with a neutral, male, English accent. The sound seemed to emanate from within the chest of the machine, as its badly damaged mouth did not appear to move. To Rory, this made the decrepit thing seem even creepier than it had before.

'Doctor. Can you hear me?' it said.

The Doctor nodded, as best he could with the thing still grabbing hold of him. 'Yes, I can hear you.'

'I do not have long before this residual power is gone and the remnants of my mind decay. I have waited a thousand years in the water for you to come, conserving what strength I had left. I have a warning for you.'

'Go on,' said the Doctor, darkly. 'I'm listening.'

'The Squall are coming. Gradius's experimental ship has torn a hole in time and the hive is manifesting in the past. Everyone is in grave danger. You told me...' The remains of the AI slumped forward, its fingers loosening on the Doctor's jacket as its voice became nothing but a long, grating drone. The Doctor caught the machine as it crumpled, laying it down gently upon the pallet. Its strange, half-rotten face stared up at them, unmoving.

The Doctor sat back, an unreadable expression on his face. Amy went to his side, kneeling on the ground beside him. She put her hand gently on the outer casing of the machine, and then jumped back as it suddenly shifted again, its hand scrabbling over the side of skid, scraping on the ground. 'And Doc... tor...' Its voice was once again a dull, metallic hiss. 'Don't forget... to... modulate... th... frequency.'

The light in the machine's eye blinked out, and all was quiet.

'Doctor? What's going on?' Amy sounded uneasy, as if what the AI had said to the Doctor had robbed her of her earlier exuberance.

'I don't know, Amy, but I'm sure it has something to do with the reason the TARDIS brought us here.'

Rory stepped forward. 'Can't you find an

alternative power source, Doctor? Plug the AI into the TARDIS and reactivate it so you can hear the rest of what it had to say?'

The Doctor shook his head. 'No. It used the last of its power to speak. Now that reserve has been spent, there's nothing left to hold its mind together. Its neural matrix will have already collapsed.' He got to his feet, dusting himself down. 'We'll just have to get to the bottom of it ourselves.'

'It was about to say something that it claimed you'd told it. But how could that be right? How could you have told it something?' Amy was wearing a puzzled expression as she grabbed the Doctor's arm and used it to hoist herself up beside him.

The Doctor shrugged. 'It must have been referring to something that hasn't happened yet. For me, at least. The AI's past, my future. That sort of thing.' He tugged at his hair in thought.

'And what about all that stuff about Gradius and a hole in time? It said everyone was in grave danger.' Amy glanced at Rory, and he tried to offer her a reassuring smile.

'Ah, well, that's a lot clearer. Someone in this period has been conducting experiments with time. It looks as if they sent an experimental ship back a thousand years, taking this AI with them. Something must have happened and it's been in the water ever since. Waiting for us.' The Doctor seemed suddenly animated now, as he began to unpick at things, teasing the meaning out of what little the AI had said.

'But why is that dangerous?' asked Rory. 'You go travelling through time and space all the time.' He glanced over at Patricia Young, who he suddenly remembered, with a cringe, was still standing nearby. Her face was stony and unreadable. She was watching the Doctor with suspicion. Rory could tell from her expression that she no longer believed they were representatives of the city conservation board, if, indeed, she ever had.

The Doctor, however, barely seemed to notice. He was too wrapped up in his thoughts. 'Rory, Rory!' he said, pacing back and forth. 'You can't just go blithely swanning about the universe, cutting great swathes through time. My people learned that long ago, and they worked out a way to manipulate the Vortex safely, to pass through without leaving great rents in their wake. There are things out there in the darkness, lurking outside of the universe, waiting to find a way in.'

'The Squall,' said Amy.

'The Squall,' the Doctor confirmed, nodding. 'Amongst others.'

'What are they?' asked Rory.

'The Squall are a race of parasites, creatures that cling to a paltry existence outside the realms of normal time and space, always looking for a means to get to the gooey core of the physical universe where you and I exist.' The Doctor mashed his hands together as he said the words 'gooey core', and Rory couldn't help thinking of the fondant centre of a chocolate egg. 'The Squall feed on psychic energy, absorbing it to establish new hives. They spread like a plague, a contagion of the whole universe. And if they are not stopped they will strip the Earth clean…'

'Then what do we have to do?' said Amy, showing signs of her usual resilience. 'Where do we find these Squall creatures?'

The Doctor shook his head. 'You, Amy Pond, are staying exactly where you are. Here, in the twenty-eighth century.'

'But—'

'No buts! No questions!' He wagged his finger dramatically. 'The Squall are extremely dangerous and they need to be stopped. I'm taking the TARDIS back to… um…' He paused to run the sonic screwdriver over the remains of the AI before examining the readout. 'The sixteenth of October 1910. The day before this sorry specimen met its end in the water. You and Rory need to find this Gradius fellow and put a stop to these experiments he's been carrying out. Whatever happens, he can't go tearing more holes in the universe. There's no use me patching things up in 1910 if more dimensional holes are going to start popping up left, right and centre. If the Squall manage to infest any more time periods they'll gain a foothold in this universe. There's no time to waste. You need to stop Gradius as a matter of urgency. Got that?'

'Got it,' said Amy, grinning. 'Come on, Rory. Let's go and see what the twenty-eighth century has to offer.'

Rory couldn't help feeling a little apprehensive about the sudden change of plan. 'Doctor, what if something happens to you in 1910? Won't Amy and I end up stuck here with no way of getting home?' Rory tried to ignore the sharp elbow he received in the ribs from his wife for his trouble.

'Rory, would I let you down?' The Doctor grinned, with a look that Rory imagined was meant to inspire great confidence. 'I'll be back before you know it. A quick hop to 1910, plug the dimensional hole, find a way to get rid of the monsters... You won't even know I've been gone.'

Rory did his best to give a winning smile, but he didn't feel particularly reassured as Amy dragged him away.

'And you, Ms Young,' said the Doctor, beaming and spinning about to face Patricia, who was now standing with a small group of archaeologists and divers, watching the exchange between the Doctor and his companions with some interest. 'I'm pleased to report that the city conservation board are satisfied with everything you're doing here.' He waved his hand to indicate the remains of the AI as he started off toward the TARDIS at a run. 'Please do carry on.'

Patricia Young, shaking her head, watched him go with a bemused expression on her face. 'Come on, boys,' she said after a minute, resignedly. 'Let's get this thing back to the lab.'

Chapter

2

London, 16 October 1910

Professor Archibald Angelchrist had yet to see one of the creatures for himself, but he'd read the descriptions in the police reports and he knew, beyond a shadow of a doubt, that they were real. The newspapers, of course, told a different story, attributing the recent rash of disappearances to the work of a serial killer or a criminal organisation. They argued that the rumours about the creatures were simply that – rumours, started by those responsible to create a climate of fear and to throw the police off their trail.

Angelchrist knew from experience, however, that most criminals were not that clever, and even those who were would be unlikely to go about blaming unearthly demons for their handiwork. No, Angelchrist wholeheartedly believed in monsters.

He knew they existed, because he'd encountered their like before.

He'd been retired for five long, quiet years now, but before that, before he'd been put out to pasture, he'd worked for the secret service as a scientific adviser, and as such he'd been party to all sorts of information about the various alien incursions that had plagued the country over the years. From the earliest surviving records, the history of Britain was a colourful account of the battles that had been lost and won against foes both human and alien. Angelchrist himself had fought against such unnatural interlopers on more than one occasion – strange tentacled things that had clambered out of the Thames; people possessed by an apparently extraterrestrial virus that drove them murderously insane; ancient entities awoken from their tombs beneath Edinburgh. Of course, the truth of such matters had been kept from the public in the interests of their own protection, but nevertheless, Angelchrist was well aware of the reality: that monsters lurked around every corner, that the universe teemed with life, and that the human race was not, as it seemed to consider itself, at the centre of everything.

It had come as no great surprise to Angelchrist then to discover that London was being slowly overrun by this new breed of demon: tall, bipedal creatures that left their victims lying in the gutters weeping blood. What concerned him most, though, was the fact that nobody seemed to be doing anything about it.

It was with that in mind that he had taken it upon himself to investigate the matter.

He knew he was no spring chicken – that he was most definitely past his prime – but his grey moustache was still peppered with traces of its original raven-black, and he was still fit and mobile. And besides, he had experience on his side.

He'd started by mapping the attacks and sightings that had been reported over the course of the previous few days, pinning them up on the laboratory wall. It had become immediately clear to him that the police were already barking up the wrong tree. They had gotten into their heads that whoever – or whatever – was responsible for the attacks, was working alone. Angelchrist could tell from the pattern of the incidents, however, that they were wrong. There were at least three of the creatures on the loose. What was more, they seemed to be behaving in a territorial fashion, maintaining their own hunting grounds distinct from one another.

Consequently, he had selected one of those territories – the area between Hyde Park and the river – and now stood on Cheyne Walk in the dusk, watching, waiting. He knew if he were patient, he would see it. A number of the bodies had been discovered in the area, and if he set himself up as bait, as easy prey, surely it would come for him. It would certainly get a surprise when it did.

The night was drawing in now, though, and Angelchrist was growing cold. The swirling fog that had been threatening to descend on the city all afternoon was finally beginning to settle; long, ghostly fingers wrapping themselves around street lamps and the masts of boats moored in the river. The moon was a bright bauble hanging low overhead, and his breath was fogging as he leaned heavily on his cane. Another hour and he'd have to head home to Grosvenor Square. Even inside his gloves, his fingers were beginning to grow numb, and his long, black overcoat and hat were offering little protection from the penetrating chill.

Angelchrist turned at the sound of footsteps in the distance. He stiffened, imagining the creature lurking there unseen, but then he heard the bark of a man's drunken laughter, and realised it was probably a crewman from one of the boats returning to his bunk. He turned back to the river, sighing with a mixture of disappointment and relief, and that was when he saw it, looming out of the fog a short distance from where he was standing.

It was just as he'd imagined it from the descriptions: tall, gangly and angular, with a slightly elongated head and a face that resembled that of a bat. Its flesh was grey and smooth, and its hands terminated in vicious claws that twitched in anticipation of what was to come. Beneath its arms hung loose flaps of skin – membranes, he presumed, for enabling it to glide through the air.

This particular specimen, however, was currently on foot, and as it came towards him, baring its fangs, Angelchrist knew that he was going to have to put up an exceptionally good fight. He raised his cane and brandished it before him like a sword, as if warning the creature to keep back. It snarled like an animal in response, and it occurred to Angelchrist that the thing wasn't necessarily blessed with intelligence or self-awareness. That, of course, made it even more of a dangerous foe. It would fight like a ravenous animal for all it was worth.

The creature stalked forward, its red eyes blazing, and Angelchrist swung his cane, levelling a blow at the side of its head. The creature shrieked in fury, but its reactions were lightning fast and it brushed aside his attack with a sweep of its arm. Angelchrist stepped back, trying to buy himself some more time. All he needed to do was knock it unconscious. A few stiff blows to the head would do it, he was sure.

He raised his arm and swung at the beast again, this time throwing all of his weight behind the motion. The cane struck home with a loud thud and the creature staggered back, shaking its head as if attempting to clear the disorientation caused by the blow. Angelchrist pressed forward, hoping to capitalise on his success, but the creature reared up again, swiping at him with its talons. They slashed through the front of his coat, scattering buttons and shreds of fabric across the cobbled road.

'Get back, beast!' Angelchrist bellowed, lurching forward with a roundhouse punch that connected squarely with the creature's jaw. It would have been enough to fell a man but the creature reeled for only a moment before its long, bony fingers whipped out and closed around Angelchrist's throat. He choked and tried to kick at the thing, but it was agile and avoided his frantic attempts to take its legs out from beneath it.

The fingers tightened around his throat, but worse, Angelchrist could feel the creature doing something else to him, somehow probing around inside his mind, as if it were sifting through his memories, tugging at them, trying to prise them free. He felt tears running down his cheeks and realised it was warm blood, trickling from the corners of his eyes. Enraged, he raised his cane and lashed out at the beast, striking it hard across the temple. Its grip on his throat loosened for a second and he pressed his advantage, shoving it forcefully back and striking it repeatedly, intent on dazing it.

It was at that point, just as Angelchrist was beginning to gain the upper hand, that a tall, thin man in a tweed jacket came barrelling out of a nearby alleyway, skidded to a halt a few steps away and raised some sort of bizarre glowing device above his head. 'Don't worry,' he called. 'I've got everything under control!'

He marched forward in the direction of the beast, waving his contraption in the air as if it were a magic wand and he a conjurer casting an enchantment to dispel the beast. Angelchrist realised the device was emitting an unusual buzzing sound.

Whatever the man was doing, it worked, for almost immediately the creature began to back away, clutching its hands to the sides of its head. Angelchrist raised his cane as if to strike it again, but he wasn't quick enough, and before he could make his move the creature had fled, hurtling away along the street. He lowered his cane in frustration.

The other man sidled over to him, looking pleased with himself. 'Hello,' he said, beaming. 'I'm the Doctor.'

Angelchrist watched with dismay as the creature made off into the night. 'No! What are you doing? Are you mad?' He took a few steps forward as if to go after the creature, but stopped when he realised it was already too late. He watched it dive over the side of the embankment, disappearing from view for a moment before rising up again on the zephyrs, sailing away into the foggy night on its membranous wings.

'Beautiful creatures, the Squall,' the Doctor said, coming to stand beside him. 'But quite deadly. Especially if there's more than one of them.'

Angelchrist turned to regard this strange, gawky man who had appeared out of nowhere to foil his plans. 'You fool!' he said, trying to bite back his frustration. 'I almost had it!'

'You almost had it? What… you mean… No! You weren't trying to catch that thing, were you?' said the Doctor, sounding impressed.

'I most certainly was,' replied Angelchrist hotly. 'And I would have managed it too, if you hadn't intervened with your strange contraption.' He sighed, attempting to compose himself. He supposed the fellow had only been trying to help. 'I imagine I owe you an apology for the brusqueness of my tone. Thank you for your assistance.'

'You're very welcome,' said the Doctor. 'I admire your bravery, Mr...?'

'Professor Angelchrist.'

'... Professor Angelchrist, but you really don't want to get on the wrong side of one of those creatures. It'll suck out all of your psychic energy before you know it. Oh... look, you're bleeding. Here.' The Doctor produced a handkerchief from his jacket pocket with a flourish, and then promptly dropped it on the ground. He looked down as it settled in a brackish puddle. 'Ah. Right. Well... yes. You might want to take a look.' He made circles beneath his eyes with his two forefingers.

Angelchrist looked the stranger up and down appraisingly. There was something odd about him. His eyes were fiercely bright and intelligent, and he obviously knew what he was talking about, but his manner was... unusual, to say the least. He was young and carried himself with a certain awkwardness, like a child who had only recently learned to walk.

Angelchrist took a handkerchief from his own pocket and dabbed at his cheeks. The Doctor had been right – he'd definitely been bleeding, just like the victims he'd seen described in the police reports. He wiped his eyes. Thankfully it seemed to have stopped.

'You're lucky it didn't have time to do any lasting harm,' the Doctor continued. He was watching Angelchrist with interest. 'A few seconds longer and you'd have been dead.' He rubbed his hand over his chin in thought. 'Still, something's not right. Something's wrong with this picture.' He frowned, leaning in and studying Angelchrist's face a little too closely for comfort, as if he expected to find the answer hidden in the lines on the man's face. Then, a moment later, his face lit up in apparent jubilation. He clicked his fingers. 'Yes! That's it! I know what's wrong. You threw me there, for a minute, professor.' He was grinning, now, like the cat that got the proverbial cream.

'What are you going on about, Doctor? What's wrong?' Angelchrist was more perplexed than outraged by the Doctor's bumbling familiarity.

The Doctor's expression changed, suddenly serious. 'I'll tell you what's wrong, professor. You're not scared. And you should be scared. You should be very, *very* scared.'

Angelchrist was momentarily taken aback by the sudden alteration in tone. 'Well... I... Look here, young man! I'll have you know I've encountered more beasts of that sort than you've had hot dinners!'

The Doctor laughed, heartily. 'Oh, I sincerely doubt that, professor. But good on you! Good for you! Getting stuck in there.' He punched Angelchrist gently on the arm, and then looked vaguely embarrassed.

'Who are you, Doctor?' asked Angelchrist.

The Doctor smiled, and his eyes seemed to flash in the moonlight. 'I'm the one the monsters are scared of,' he said, cryptically, and Angelchrist didn't detect even a hint of irony.

'You're not from around here, are you?' said Angelchrist.

'Ah, now that's a long story,' the Doctor replied. 'A good one, admittedly, filled with lots of gadding about and danger and adventure, but very long, and it's cold out here. And besides, it's far more important you tell me why you were trying to catch that thing.'

'What was it you called it?' asked Angelchrist.

'A Squall. An alien from another dimensional plane. A parasite with an insatiable appetite for psychic energy.' The Doctor brushed his hair from his eyes. 'It certainly wouldn't have taken kindly to being put in a cage. It wouldn't have proved any less dangerous, either.'

Angelchrist shrugged. 'Someone needs to do something. To stop them. People are dying, and Scotland Yard is still saying it's the work of a serial killer. During my time in the secret service I fought to protect the country from incursions such as this. I thought if I could catch it, I could study it, find out what they were. Prove to the police once and for all what it was they were up against. I've been mapping the pattern of their attacks. There are three of them, I believe, each of them keeping to its own territory within the boundaries of the city.'

The Doctor smiled. 'I fear, professor, there are far more of them than that. The Squall are hive creatures, like ants or bees. Their numbers will be growing with every passing hour as more and more of them spill through the rent in the universe that brought them here.' The Doctor tapped his mechanical contraption idly in the palm of his hand. 'You say you've been mapping the location of their attacks?'

'Indeed…'

'Then I need you to show me. As soon as you can. It could be of critical importance.' The Doctor turned and set off in the direction he had come. After a few steps he stopped and turned back, gesturing up and down the street. 'Umm, lead on!' He looked at Angelchrist sheepishly, and shrugged. 'I don't know the way.'

Angelchrist knew that he should walk away from this strange man, should simply thank him for his assistance and leave. But there was something about him, about the intensity in his eyes, about the way he seemed to know exactly what was going on, that compelled Angelchrist to trust him. He had the notion that the Doctor could help him get to the bottom of the situation with the Squall. He didn't know exactly where the Doctor had come from, but he supposed it didn't matter. Not if he could help Angelchrist to prevent any further deaths.

'This way, Doctor,' he said, pointing in the opposite direction with the end of his cane. 'I have a motor car parked around the corner and my house is only a short drive away. I'd be happy to help.'

The Doctor grinned. 'I'm glad to hear that, Professor Angelchrist,' he said. 'Good choice.'

Chapter

3

London, 10 June 2789

It had taken Amy and Rory the best part of a day to navigate their way through the teeming streets of the metropolis.

London had changed almost beyond recognition, as unfamiliar to Rory as any alien world. Some of the landmarks were the same, of course: St Paul's Cathedral still sat squat and proud by Ludgate Hill; the Tower of London, now unimaginably old, remained like a sentry by the river; Buckingham Palace had been preserved almost as it had been in Amy and Rory's time. These familiar monuments were not enough, however, to dispel the sense of dislocation, the feeling that they were somewhere else, somewhere that wasn't London. It felt to Rory as if those ancient buildings had somehow been plucked from where they had sat, back home in the twenty-first century, and dropped here in this other time and place, in the middle of a different city, on a different world. Given the things he'd seen with the Doctor, he knew that wasn't as outlandish an idea as it sounded.

Amy, ever the more streetwise one, had led the way, but even she had been enchanted by the sheer magic of the place, unable to wipe the look of wide-eyed wonder from her face. Rory had squeezed her hand and held on to her as they'd fought their way through the milling crowds, past strange-looking boutiques staffed by talking computer terminals and restaurants selling a bizarre mix of dishes, from the almost incongruously traditional shepherd's pie to the unpalatable sounding 'corobian scuff'.

Rory had expected to see flying cars and hoverboards and all that stuff from *Back to the Future*, but in reality, the city was still just a city, as unfamiliar as it was. There did appear to be a version of the Tube still in operation – a system of pneumatic trains that shot soundlessly through a network of tunnels beneath the city – but they had chosen to walk in order to drink in the sights. Or rather, Amy had insisted on it.

At one point they had turned down what had seemed like a familiar side road just off Oxford Street, only to come across the base of one of the large domes they had seen from the other side of the river. It appeared to erupt from the ground itself, a towering wall of shimmering crystal, curving up into the sky and away in all directions; a vast bubble of glass in the centre of the metropolis.

To Rory it had looked like an enormous version of one of those botanical experiments, a micro-ecology in a bottle, but the area it covered must have been half a square mile, all the way down to the river's edge. Huge swathes of the old city must have been cleared away to accommodate it.

Amy had pressed herself up against the glass, her hands cupped to her face so she could peer at the strange, bottled environment inside. It was utterly at odds with the city around them: instead of tall towers of steel and glass or the crumbling monuments of ages past, the dome contained what appeared to be a lush, green forest, complete with brazenly coloured birds and a lioness stalking through the undergrowth, only a few metres away from where they were standing. Inside, at the apex of the dome, Rory had noticed a bank of huge fans mounted on a series of steel frames.

'What do you think it is?' Rory had said, thinking aloud. 'Some sort of zoo or conservation area?'

Amy had shaken her head. 'Perhaps. More likely it's an oxygen factory like the one at the heart of the *Byzantium*.' She'd shuddered as she'd said this, stepping back from the glass wall. 'Big city, no trees, lots of people. I reckon this is how they keep everyone breathing.'

Rory had been impressed by her deduction. Clearly all that time spent with the Doctor was beginning to rub off on her. 'An oxygen factory…' he'd said, bewildered. He didn't like the implication of that, what it suggested had happened to the

Earth's natural habitats in the intervening centuries since their own time.

They'd moved on, dazzled by the strangeness of this future London, frustrated by the things that hadn't changed. Rory had caught sight of more than one of the artificial people – what he assumed to be the 'nearly human' AIs that Patricia Young had referred to, just like the one they'd pulled out of the river. Except, of course, these examples were up and about, sheathed in pale, rubbery skin, walking along beside their owners. They were fetching, carrying and otherwise assisting their rich benefactors, as if they were nothing but personal butlers. Some of them were even dressed in the typical apparel of an Edwardian servant, all black suits and white gloves. Something about it just didn't sit right with Rory. He didn't like the notion of slaves, whether they were human or machine.

Neither of them had really known where to start in their search for Gradius. They didn't even know – they realised as they set about their task – if they were looking for a man or a woman.

At first they'd decided to try to locate any institutes or establishments at which a leading scientist might be conducting experiments such as the Doctor had described, but that had led them down a blind alley. Literally, on at least one occasion. So, instead, they had wandered the streets, trying to get their bearings, wracking their brains for a way to narrow their search. Rory had even tried getting his mobile phone to connect to a network in order to run a search on the name 'Gradius', but, of course, his service provider had long ago ceased to exist, the technology having become entirely obsolete. He'd wondered if people even had mobile phones in the future. Or, indeed, whether the internet had been superseded by something entirely new.

In the end, however, the answer had been almost ridiculously simple.

Amy had pointed out one of the tall, black boxes that seemed to pepper the streets, installed at intervals all over the city. They were coffin-shaped and around two and a half metres tall, hollow and open-fronted. Rory had pretty much ignored them as they'd passed them by, distracted by the sheer magnificence of the view, too busy looking all around him to worry about what these strange, box-like constructions really were.

What Amy had seen, however, was a person stepping into one, just across the street. Rory had watched with interest as the man had disappeared inside and a faint blue light had emanated from within the box. Moments later, voices had followed. It was at that moment he'd realised what the black boxes actually were.

'Information terminals,' he'd said, turning to Amy with a wide grin on his face, only to see her already dashing off down the street toward another, unoccupied booth. Sighing, he'd followed after her.

He'd caught up with her a few seconds later, just as she was entering the box. 'Amy, don't you think we should—'

'Sshhh,' she'd replied, cutting him off, as a holographic image had flickered into being in the dark recess at the back of the booth: an electronic ghost with a blank, hairless, asexual face. Only its head and shoulders were visible, giving Rory the impression that it was leaning forward from the shadowy recess, dipping its head into the light.

Rory had watched over Amy's shoulder, straining to get a proper look at what was happening. The holographic face had stared at them impassively for a moment, and then it had spoken. 'Welcome to the City of London. I am your guide. How may I be of assistance?'

'Erm… We're trying to find someone?' Amy had said, with a shrug.

'Please state the name of the person you wish to locate,' the hologram had replied in cool, unemotional tones.

'Gradius,' Amy had continued, glancing over her shoulder at Rory with a cheeky smile, her eyes wide with excitement, as if to say '*this is the future, Rory!*' He couldn't help but grin back in return. Her enthusiasm was utterly infectious.

'There are six occurrences of the name Gradius in the directory,' the hologram had stated after a moment, and a list of names and addresses had scrolled up before Amy, the glowing letters apparently hovering in mid air.

'Look! There! A Professor C. Gradius. That has to be the one we're looking for,' Rory had said, pointing to the name.

'Well, the professor bit does kind of give the game away there, bright spark,' Amy had laughed, before reaching out and tentatively prodding at the name with an outstretched index finger.

Rory had felt her start as the holographic face had suddenly dispersed in a shower of glittering fragments, and in its place a map had resolved, showing them the location of the professor's workshop or home, indicated by a blinking light. Beneath the map, the address scrolled through the air, the letters shining a bright, holographic blue.

'This is the registered address of Professor C. Gradius. Currently, the professor does not appear to be in residence,' the disembodied voice of the guide had announced.

Rory had thought it sounded a little bored, but he could have been imagining it. Surely, he'd considered, holographic guides couldn't actually *get* bored?

'I know where that is,' Amy had said. 'It's right near the British Museum. Look, there it is on the map. I visited it once when I was a kid.'

'It should be easy enough to find,' Rory had agreed. 'It's only about half an hour's walk from here. I think.'

'Um, thank you,' Amy had said to the guide, backing out of the booth.

'Enjoy your stay in London,' the monotone voice had replied, and the two of them had set out with a renewed sense of purpose.

Now, they stood on the threshold of a large,

modern-looking building about ten minutes' walk from the British Museum. The frontage was all steel and glass, and through the towering windows Rory could see a curved reception desk in the sparsely furnished lobby.

'It looks like a hotel,' he said, peering inside.

'Do you think anyone actually lives here?' Amy replied, trying the door handle. It turned easily in her hand and the door creaked open.

'I think we're about to find out,' said Rory, ushering her in through the opening.

Inside, the building smelled of polish. That was the only way Rory could describe it. Clean, clinical – the sort of smell that got right up your nose and lingered there for hours. The place itself was immaculate. The marble floor gleamed in the reflected light of the overhead strip lights, the walls were bare and white, and the sweeping lines of the reception desk were hewn from a single piece of black granite. Upon it the legend GRADIUS INDUSTRIES was emblazed in foot-high letters. So, it was an office or laboratory, after all.

Across the lobby was a spiral staircase leading to both upper and lower floors, designed to represent the twisting lattices of a double helix. Someone had spent a *lot* of money on the interior design.

'There's no one here,' he said, redundantly. It was cold, and he had the oddest sense that something here was very wrong. 'Where's the receptionist?'

Amy shrugged. 'Probably another of those holographic whatjamacallits,' she said, strolling pointedly over to the desk, her boots clopping on the polished stone floor.

'There's no muzak, either,' Rory muttered. 'Places like this *always* have muzak.'

'Are you telling me you'd *rather* have some dodgy instrumental rendition of a Justin Bieber song?'

Rory gave his best *'what do you take me for'* look, but she only smiled sweetly and turned to lean on the reception desk. 'Helloooo?' she called. 'Anyone at home?'

There was no reply.

'Helloooo?' she tried again.

Rory glanced at the stairs, then back at the door. 'Look, it's pretty clear no one's here. Perhaps we got the wrong place?' He was starting to feel increasingly uncomfortable.

Amy frowned. 'No, that can't be right. There has to be someone here.'

'Even that holographic thing out there told us Professor Gradius wasn't at home. We shouldn't be in here,' Rory said, half turning toward the door.

'If nobody's at home, why was the door open?' Amy asked, and Rory knew she had a point. 'Besides, there's a *reception desk*. It's not like we're trespassing in someone's house.' She clopped over to him and took his hand. 'Come on. I think we should take a look around.'

'I've got a bad feeling about this, Amy…'

'Oh, come on! Where's your sense of adventure!' She beamed at him and he felt himself giving in, despite his sense of impending danger.

'I suppose we did promise the Doctor…' he said.

'Precisely! So…' she took his hand and dragged him across the lobby towards the staircase, 'upstairs or downstairs first?'

'Um…' Rory peered up and down the stairwell. It looked more than a little precarious. 'Upstairs,' he said, with confidence. 'We should look upstairs first.'

'Great,' Amy said, jumping onto the steps and beginning her descent to the lower level.

'I said upstairs first!' said Rory, as she took the metal rungs two at a time.

'Exactly!' was the only response he received, her voice drifting back up the stairwell, already halfway down the flight to the lower level.

Shaking his head he followed behind her, wondering – not for the first time – at how often he seemed to do just that.

'What did you mean, "exactly"?'

'You should take it as a compliment. I'm trusting your instincts.'

'My instincts told me we should look upstairs, just as I said.'

'Precisely. Which is why I figured we should look downstairs first. Your gut was telling you to avoid the dark, scary hangar that you expected us to find down here. And that's exactly the sort of place we *should* be looking.'

Rory frowned. Somehow, however wrong it

seemed on the surface, he couldn't argue with Amy's logic. 'Well, I suppose I can see your point. Kind of.'

She elbowed him affectionately in the ribs. 'See. Trusting your instincts. And now look,' she gave an expansive gesture with her arms, 'a big, scary hangar. The Doctor would be so proud.'

They were standing at the bottom of the stairs in what appeared to be a very large open space. Rory could discern as much from the way their voices echoed, and from the fact the light seeping down from the stairwell did absolutely nothing to dispel the darkness that seemed to close in on them from all sides.

'So... definitely not a hotel,' he said.

Amy shook her head as she walked cautiously forward into the gloom. 'It must be some sort of underground warehouse or workshop,' she said.

'Yes. And Professor Gradius definitely isn't here,' he replied.

Amy took another step forward and there was a sudden, stuttering flash of light. Rory blinked and covered his face with the back of his hand to ward off the glare. Banks of brilliant electric bulbs blinked on in sudden succession, flooding the hangar with sickly yellow light, triggered – he guessed – by Amy's movements.

'That's more like it!' exclaimed Amy.

Rory peered between his fingers while he waited for his eyes to adjust to the sudden alteration in their surroundings. The hangar was as big as he'd imagined – bigger, even – and was lined with workbenches and computer stations, banks of monitors and pools of cables. Wires trailed from the ceiling like writhing vipers dripping from the branches of trees, and beneath them, right in the centre of the room, sat a huge, shining, silver spaceship. At least, to Rory, it looked like a spaceship. It was like something out of a science fiction film, a gleaming escape pod or shuttlecraft, the sort of thing he would have expected to see filling the skies over London in the twenty-eighth century, if he hadn't been there to know otherwise.

The ship was around fifteen metres in length and about the height of an average car. It appeared to be fashioned from panels of shining chrome or polished steel, gleaming in the harsh, reflected light. It was shaped like a lozenge with a conical nose, and a hatchway was open in one side of it like a gull's wing. Some of the overhead cables actually snaked down and disappeared inside the machine like fat umbilical cords, plugged into sockets on its outer shell.

Rory drifted towards it without really noticing what he was doing. 'Just look at it,' he said. 'Do you think this is the time machine the Doctor was talking about? It doesn't look that experimental.'

Amy shrugged. 'Must be,' she said, walking slowly around it, reaching out to run her fingers over its smooth surface.

'Careful,' said Rory. 'Do you think you should be touching that?'

Amy, however, had stopped dead in her tracks and was staring at something by her feet, an expression of absolute horror on her face. Rory ran to her side without a moment's hesitation. 'Amy? Are you…' He trailed off when he saw what she was looking at.

Lying there on the stone floor, in the shadow of the time machine, was a pretty woman in her early thirties. She was wearing a white lab coat and her blonde hair was tied back in a severe ponytail. Her face, however, was twisted into a visage of utter terror, and dark, sticky tributaries stained her cheeks and collar.

She was dead, and she had died weeping blood.

Chapter
4

London, 16 October 1910

Angelchrist's laboratory was full of wonders. Or so he liked to think. He loved the room and spent most of his time within its four walls, more so now, ironically, that he'd been forced to retire from active duty. He lived alone – he always had – and wasn't yet ready to idle away his days with his pipe and slippers.

So, instead, Angelchrist put his time to good use in the lab, working on some of the inventions he'd always intended to develop, studying rare specimens of plant and animal life, unofficially investigating crimes that Scotland Yard seemed unable to satisfactorily handle. As a consequence the room was brimming with all manner of paraphernalia: a human skeleton, the skull of a great cat, a large clockwork orrery, a case of ancient, leather-bound books, maps pasted to the walls, photographs of the catacombs beneath Edinburgh, the case of an Egyptian mummy, a cabinet filled with trophies – the list went on.

Angelchrist set the tea tray down upon the table and turned to see what the Doctor was doing. For a moment he couldn't see him amongst the chaotic forest of artefacts, but then he spotted him over in the corner of the laboratory, examining some of the machinery.

Angelchrist smiled. The Doctor was running his strange device over one of the professor's most prized possessions: a clockwork owl, given to him years ago by an old and very dear friend. The Doctor turned when he heard Angelchrist approaching.

'What is that marvellous contraption, Doctor?'

'This?' The Doctor held it out, still bent low, studying the owl. 'This is a sonic screwdriver.'

Angelchrist took it and turned it over in his hands. 'A screwdriver?' he said, handing it back to the Doctor, a little unimpressed. 'I've always believed in the principle that tools shouldn't be over-engineered. I mean, why go to all of that trouble when a traditional screwdriver would do the job just as well?' He shrugged. 'Still, I suppose we're lucky that Squall didn't think much of the sound it was making.'

Turning around, the Doctor looked suddenly taken aback. 'Well, it's really not that simple…'

'Precisely!' replied Angelchrist.

'Oh, never mind…' said the Doctor, tucking the

sonic screwdriver back into his pocket. 'Where's this map of yours, professor?'

'Over here, on the wall.' He led the Doctor to the other end of the laboratory, avoiding the life-sized model of a Neanderthal man that stood propped against a stack of wooden crates.

'The map is a little out of date, I'm afraid, but London doesn't change all that much,' he said.

'Try telling that to Amy and Rory,' the Doctor said cryptically, distracted by the raft of artefacts that covered the workbench beside him. 'Ah, a top hat!' he said, suddenly, plucking it from where it sat atop an ancient globe and putting it on his head. 'I love top hats. Top hats are—'

'—entirely inappropriate for an occasion such as this, Doctor.'

The Doctor looked vaguely crestfallen as he removed the hat and placed it back on the workbench. His face brightened when he looked up and saw the map. 'Excellent work, professor!' He stepped closer, looking up at the yellowing old street map of London that Angelchrist had pasted to the wall. It was covered in an array of pins, each one marking the scene of one of the recent attacks or sightings. Around it, Angelchrist had pinned grainy photographs of six of the victims, each one taken in the police morgue, the victims' faces all streaked with dried tributaries of blood. Lines of string stretched from each photograph to the exact locations of their deaths.

Angelchrist still had friends in Scotland Yard,

and they were more than happy to provide him with all the information he needed, grateful as they were for his help.

'I fear the Squall have been busy, Doctor. The reported attacks have been steadily increasing in number since Thursday,' said Angelchrist, his voice low.

'Hmmm. Then there are all the *un*reported ones to consider, too,' the Doctor replied.

The Doctor stood for a moment in silence, tracing his fingers over the lines of the map, turning his head this way and that as he interpreted the data. 'There's not quite enough information to triangulate an exact position, but it looks as though the region we want is about here,' he said, tapping the map with his finger, 'somewhere around Holborn and the British Museum.'

'What exactly is it you're looking for, Doctor?' said Angelchrist, studying the map over the Doctor's shoulder.

'I need to locate the epicentre, the vessel that punched a hole in the universe and allowed the Squall to infest this time period. If I can find it I have a shot at stopping them before the hive can fully manifest.'

'What happens then? If this… hive is allowed to establish itself here?' Angelchrist decided not to bring up the bit about 'this time period' or the questions that such a statement implied.

'The end of the world,' the Doctor replied, gravely. 'The Squall will suck it dry. And once they've finished, once they've drained the human race of all its psychic energy, they'll move on. They'll use the Earth as a beachhead, a staging post from which to expand throughout the galaxy, setting up hives on innumerable worlds as they go. Within a few hundred thousand years they'll have conquered half the galactic spiral. They have to be stopped.' The Doctor fixed Angelchrist with a firm stare. 'Will you help me, professor?'

Angelchrist looked the Doctor straight in the eye. 'I'm an old man, Doctor. I'm not sure what use I can be.'

The Doctor raised a questioning eyebrow. 'Oh, I'd say you can be a great deal of use, professor, if you're up for it.' He smiled. 'Are you sure you want to miss it?'

Angelchrist couldn't hide the smile that crept onto his lips. 'One last adventure, eh, Doctor? Once more unto the breach and all that. Why not? I'd be honoured.'

The Doctor grinned. 'You're a remarkable man, professor,' he said, clapping Angelchrist on the shoulder and steering him toward the door. 'Now, we're going to need your car...'

'Overhead, professor. Have you seen them?' The Doctor had to shout over the noise of the wind as they hurtled through the streets in Angelchrist's open-topped motor car. Somehow, the Doctor had persuaded Angelchrist to let him drive, and now, bent over the wheel, his hair whipping wildly about his face, he looked every bit the madcap adventurer. Angelchrist hadn't felt so alive in years.

He looked to the skies. It was late – approaching midnight – and he could see very little for the darkness and the wispy fog. What he could discern, however, stark against the moonlight, were three Squall, circling the rooftops of the city, gliding smoothly on the shifting currents. He wondered if they were searching for prey, or whether, perhaps, they were keeping watch on something far below. If the latter were true, then the likelihood was that he and the Doctor would be spotted before they ever got near to their destination.

Whatever the case, the Doctor had been right. There were clearly more of them than Angelchrist had at first assumed. If the Doctor was to be believed – something which Angelchrist was becoming more and more disposed to do, the longer he spent with the man – there'd be many, many more to come if they couldn't find a way to close the inter-dimensional rift through which they were spilling like a torrent of living poison.

Angelchrist didn't quite understand the complexities of the situation, but he knew enough to have grasped that the Squall represented a terrible threat. If they were allowed to establish a hive in the physical world they would spread and devour every living thing they encountered, extinguishing entire species as they fuelled their insatiable appetite.

Angelchrist had always suspected the universe was teeming with life. He'd known other life forms existed, of course – he'd seen examples of them on Earth during his active years in the secret service – but to have the Doctor confirm the existence of myriad other worlds, to hear him describe the vastness of the populated universe, the near-infinite spread of life... Well, that was something else entirely. Angelchrist's world had suddenly got bigger and exceedingly more interesting, and whatever he did, he wasn't about to let these alien parasites take that away from him.

The Doctor yanked the steering wheel and the car lurched around a corner, causing Angelchrist to bounce up and down in his seat, nearly tumbling out over the low side of the door. 'Steady as she goes, Doctor! There is a brake, you know.'

The Doctor grinned but kept his eyes on the road ahead, searching intently for any sign of the vessel he expected to find in the area. 'I haven't had this much fun since Bessie!' he said cryptically.

Angelchrist still hadn't been able to ascertain exactly who the Doctor was, or where he had come from, but surprisingly he found himself happy to accept that ambiguity for now. The Doctor clearly had a sophisticated understanding of how the universe worked – much more so than anyone Angelchrist had ever met – and the intensity and urgency with which he worked had been enough to carry Angelchrist along in his wake. What surprised the professor most about this remarkable man, however, was the fact he actually appeared to be *enjoying* himself, too. There was a kind of exuberance about him, a *joie de vivre* that to Angelchrist seemed utterly infectious. No matter that they were hurtling headlong into danger – the Doctor appeared to relish every moment of it. Being with the Doctor reminded Angelchrist of his younger, carefree self, of his days of adventure and derring-do. In his eyes, that was no bad thing. It felt as if he were finally shaking off the cobwebs that had settled over him these last few years and embracing the spirit of adventure once again. The thought brought a welcome smile to his lips, and he leaned back in his seat to watch the houses flit by as they shot along the road at speed.

The streets at this time of night were near deserted, save for the odd lonely figure drifting along the pavements, making their way home from some hostelry or other, less salubrious undertaking. The Doctor paid them no heed as he sent the car careening along the roads, spinning the wheel to send them flying around corners, the headlamps bobbing as the vehicle was jolted this way and that. The twin beams seemed to burrow through the wispy fog, penetrating the gloom like shimmering arrows.

Presently, after nearly half an hour spent circling the area in the immediate vicinity of the British Museum, the Doctor brought the car to a sharp halt by the side of the road, cranking the handbrake so that the vehicle lurched dramatically before shuddering to rest. Without even so much as glancing in Angelchrist's direction he leapt up out of the driver's seat, sprang over the side of the car and produced his sonic screwdriver from his jacket pocket. He proceeded to hold it aloft like a torch, pressing the button that caused it to emit the loud buzzing noise that Angelchrist was beginning to find a little grating.

'I fail to see what a screwdriver is going to do to aid us in our search for this mysterious vessel, Doctor?' said Angelchrist, perplexed once again by the Doctor's bizarre behaviour.

The Doctor was turning about on the spot, regarding his instrument with a thoughtful expression on his face. 'Yes, I...' He trailed off, turning back on himself to face in the opposite direction. 'Ah ha! This way!' He set off at a brisk pace, and only turned to look back at Angelchrist – who was still sitting in the passenger seat – when he was already halfway along the street. 'Come on, professor!' he called, beckoning for Angelchrist to join him. 'You'll get cold sitting there.'

Laughing, despite himself, Angelchrist popped open the car door and clambered down onto the pavement. He hurried over to where the Doctor was waiting for him.

'Now, very important this next bit. Stay alert. Watch the skies as well as the streets. And most crucial of all,' the Doctor patted Angelchrist on the lapel with his sonic screwdriver as if to emphasise this last point, 'do absolutely everything I say.'

Angelchrist nodded. 'You can count on me, Doctor,' he said, fingering the butt of his revolver in his pocket.

The Doctor held his finger up in the air as if judging the direction of the wind. 'This way,' he said, and then set off at a run.

Sighing, Angelchrist gave chase. At least, he thought, all of this running about was going to keep him fit.

It didn't take the Doctor long to find what he was looking for.

Angelchrist had lost track entirely of where they were, after following the Doctor down a series of alleyways and side streets, concentrating hard on keeping up with the enigmatic stranger. It seemed to Angelchrist as if they'd already doubled back on themselves innumerable times and that the Doctor was generally working hard to get them utterly lost. He would dash down a narrow lane at a run, stop dead, consult his sonic screwdriver and then set off again in the other direction, tutting to himself and frowning.

Just as Angelchrist was becoming exasperated, as well as breathless, the Doctor ducked down another darkened alleyway, almost slipping over on the damp cobbles in his haste, the tip of his sonic screwdriver casting eerie shadows on the redbrick walls.

'If I'm right...' he announced, in a voice that suggested he thought himself to be exactly that, 'then it should be just about...' He stopped suddenly, kicked open the back gate of a terraced house and stood back, a beaming smile on his face. 'Here!'

The Doctor folded his arms across his chest, evidently pleased with himself.

'One terribly dangerous, experimental time ship that should never have been created.' He leaned forward, peering in through the opening. 'Oh, but it does look rather splendid, doesn't it? This Gradius fellow has a good eye for aesthetics, even if his applied physics is a little on the wonky side.'

Angelchrist, who up until this point had still been hurrying along, trying to keep pace with the Doctor, came to a stop by the open gate. He leaned against the wall with one hand, his breath coming in long, rasping gasps. When he turned to see what the Doctor was staring at, however, he suddenly forgot all about his aching limbs, his sore feet and the sweat beading on his brow. He stepped forward, drinking in the sight.

A gleaming silver spaceship – or what looked to Angelchrist very much like he imagined a spaceship *should* look – was partially buried in the back wall of the house. The potting shed, or what had once been the potting shed, had been reduced to nothing but a pile of rubble beneath the weight of the vessel, and broken glass from a greenhouse lay scattered all across the flagstones of the backyard.

The vessel itself seemed to shimmer in the reflected moonlight, its smooth hull unblemished by the violent manner of its arrival. It was shaped like a bulbous torpedo, about the size of three motor cars in length, and a hatchway was open in its flank like a dark, gaping maw. Clearly, the ship had disgorged someone, or some*thing*, into the yard.

What puzzled Angelchrist most of all, however, was the fact that – although the ship appeared to be half buried in the brickwork of the house – the wall itself did not seem to have been damaged by the impact. It was almost as if the building had been built around the ship, or as if the nose of the vessel had been sliced off and the fuselage pushed flush with the wall to give the impression that it had somehow grown there like a vast silver blemish, a rupture on the side of the building.

'It's… remarkable. Beautiful. It's like nothing I've ever conceived of, even in my wildest imaginings.' Angelchrist turned to the Doctor. 'Is this what the future looks like, Doctor?'

The Doctor grinned. 'This? Well, sort of, I suppose. It's actually fairly primitive, really, as far as time-capable vessels go. Looks impressive though, doesn't it?'

Angelchrist edged slowly through the opening towards the ship, his feet crunching on broken shards of glass. There was a smell in the air, like the scent of burnt ozone after a lightning storm. 'Why does it look like that, Doctor? Half in the wall, I mean.'

Angelchrist heard the Doctor follow him into the yard.

'Ah, yes. Well, that's the "experimental" part, you see. Whoever built this thing hadn't considered fitting it out with proximity alarms. It's materialised at the right coordinates, even though those coordinates were already partially occupied by a wall.'

'Meaning…?'

'Meaning the nose of the ship has materialised *inside* the wall. Luckily for the people inside the ship, the wall wasn't any thicker,' said the Doctor.

'Or any closer to the alleyway,' Angelchrist said, his voice low. He could still hardly believe what he was seeing.

The Doctor approached the remains of the crashed ship, running the palm of his hand over the silvery hull. Angelchrist could tell that, despite what he'd said about the vessel being primitive, the Doctor was genuinely impressed by the craftsmanship.

'What of this dimensional hole you spoke of, Doctor? Wasn't that the reason you wanted to find the ship in the first place?'

'Oh, that'll be somewhere close by, no doubt. Probably inside the house. Or over there, in what's left of that outside loo. Won't be much to see. Just a vague shimmer in the air where the skein between dimensions is a bit thin, like a heat haze on a road.' The Doctor hadn't taken his eyes off the vessel as he spoke. 'The thing that's worrying me, though, is why no one has noticed there's a whopping great time ship in their neighbour's backyard. I mean – look at the thing: big, shining, futuristic-looking ship. Must have appeared with a heck of a bang. We're in the middle of a terrace of what, fifty houses?' The Doctor stepped back, putting his hands on his hips, still regarding the ship.

'Ah, Doctor…?'

'You'd think someone might have noticed it by now, reported it to the police. You'd think the place would be swarming with people.'

'*Doctor!*' Angelchrist hissed, his voice growing ever more insistent as he tried to get the Doctor's attention.

'Instead, the whole street is absolutely silent. It's as if there's nobody here. All the lights are off, in all the houses… Oh.' The Doctor stopped talking suddenly, as if a light bulb had just gone on inside his head. 'And that's exactly why you're trying to get my attention, isn't it, professor? Because I've forgotten something really quite important. I've forgotten there are monsters here, lurking in the shadows.' The Doctor turned to look at Angelchrist, a pained expression on his face. 'I don't really want to look now, do I? They're here, aren't they?'

'Quite so, Doctor. I rather think you have your reason,' said Angelchrist, pointing over the Doctor's shoulder at the massing ranks of Squall. They were hanging from the eaves of the nearby houses like gargoyles, or scrabbling over the rooftops, or squatting on the walls. Their red eyes burned in the darkness like hot coals. There must have been fifty of them, at the very least, up and down the entire street. Clearly, they had made short work of any people in the vicinity of the crash site, harvesting their psychic energy to feed the hive. That was why nobody had reported the appearance of the ship – because there was nobody left here to do so.

Angelchrist started as one of the creatures swooped down from above, landing noisily on the wooden fence that separated the yard they were in from the neighbouring property. It raised its head and issued the most terrifying shriek, baring its fangs as it regarded them. Its black talons scored the wooden panels as it settled, wrapping its membranous wings around itself protectively.

'Hello,' said the Doctor brightly. 'Pleasant night for it.'

The Squall hissed at him from between its teeth.

Others were coming closer now, too, and a quick glance up at the house told Angelchrist the place was swarming with them. He could see them crowding the windows inside the house, too. One was hanging from a drainpipe just a few paces away.

Angelchrist slipped his hand into his pocket, reassured by the feel of his revolver, cold and hard against his palm.

'Oh, come on,' continued the Doctor. 'You can do better than that. There are plenty of you here now. You must have at least the intelligence of an average human between you.'

'We,' said the Squall in its thick, gravelly voice.

'Are,' said another to Angelchrist's left, which had hopped over the fence and was now stalking towards them over the rubble of the potting shed, its talons extended.

'Squall,' said the third, from its perch on a window ledge above.

'And. We. Shall. Feast,' they finished, each of

them drawling a word in turn.

'Yes, yes, yes,' said the Doctor. 'Heard it all before. Same old story. But I'm afraid that's not going to happen.'

'The. Hive. Is. Manifesting,' the Squall replied in their strange, disjointed speech, 'And. It. Hungers.'

'I understand all that. I really do. Biological imperatives, insatiable appetites, I get it. But this universe isn't for the taking. You can't have it.' He sighed. 'Look, you're intelligent enough now to understand what I'm offering you here, so I'll give you a chance. I'll give you *one* chance. Turn around and leave. All of you, now, just turn and go back to where you came from. Either that, or I'm going to have to do it for you.' He straightened his back, meeting the gaze of the Squall on the fence. 'Make you leave, that is,' he added quietly.

Angelchrist could hardly believe the manner in which the Doctor was speaking to the monstrous creatures. Every fibre in his body screamed at him to start shooting at the things, to take as many of them down as he could before they descended on him and began tearing him apart. But it was as if the Doctor wasn't scared of them, as if he did this sort of thing all the time. There was a kind of weary inevitability about the way he addressed them, as if he knew that the Squall were never going to accept his offer, but felt obliged to make it anyway.

'This. World. Is. So. Rich,' the Squall continued, unperturbed by the Doctor's threat. 'And. You… We. Can. Smell. You… We. Shall. Feast. On. You.'

Angelchrist saw the Doctor's shoulders sag.

The professor stepped forward, pulling his revolver from his pocket and brandishing it before him. 'Have you any weapons, Doctor?'

The Doctor turned to Angelchrist, and the professor was momentarily taken aback by the coldness he saw in the Doctor's eyes. 'Put your gun away, professor. You won't be needing it,' he said, severely.

Angelchrist frowned. 'But...' he started, before trailing off. He'd promised the Doctor he'd do exactly as asked, and he would be true to his word, as much as it pained him. He slipped the revolver back into his pocket. He hoped that whatever the Doctor had up his sleeve, it was good.

There was a sudden screeching sound from somewhere to his right, accompanied by the sound of claws grating on metal, and both Angelchrist and the Doctor turned to see another of the creatures emerging from the hatchway of the ship, something soft and red draped in its claws. It was an article of clothing, as far as Angelchrist could tell, some sort of jumper with a hood.

'Amy!' the Doctor yelled, rushing forward and snatching the item from the Squall's grasp. It tore as he wrenched it free, and the alien shrieked, raising its claws to attack. The Doctor, his face like thunder, wrenched his sonic screwdriver from his pocket and held it aloft. 'If you've hurt her...' he said, and there was real ire in his voice. 'If you've hurt her, then you'd better hope you've manifested a whole army by the time I return. Because that's the only thing that will stop me. Mark my words.'

He depressed the button on his sonic screwdriver and all around them the Squall began screeching in pain and scratching violently at their heads. The creature immediately in front the Doctor buckled to its knees on the ground, wrapping its membranous wings around itself and burying its head in its arms as if trying to blot out the sound. Further afield, along the street, the unaffected creatures looked on curiously, as if unable to understand what had suddenly become of their kin. Angelchrist realised they must have been out of range of the Doctor's device.

Still holding his screwdriver aloft, the Doctor turned and tossed Angelchrist the jumper he'd taken from the creature, and then ducked his head into the hatch of the ship. He remained there for a moment or two as if looking for something. Then, stepping back from the vessel, he walked over to where Angelchrist was standing, wide-eyed with wonder.

'I can't keep this up for long,' said the Doctor, motioning with the sonic screwdriver. 'It'll drain all the power. And besides, the hive adapts quickly. Within a few minutes they'll have figured out how to filter out the sound. Better to conserve what we can for later.' He searched Angelchrist's face for understanding. 'We might need it,' he added.

Angelchrist nodded.

'So, when I take my finger off this button...' said the Doctor.

'More running?' asked Angelchrist, with a grin.

'More running,' the Doctor replied, but the smile was gone from his face, replaced instead by a haunted expression that sent a cold shiver running down Angelchrist's spine. 'They're going to be very, very angry,' he said. 'Are you ready?'

Angelchrist turned back to see the Squall still writhing on the ground, or screaming from their perches, clinging on as they twisted and turned in agony at the frequency being emitted by the Doctor's sonic screwdriver. The sound of their anguish was at once terrifying and moving. 'I'm ready.'

The Doctor nodded. 'Then run!' he bellowed, as they both hurtled toward the alleyway, a pack of baying alien parasites hot on their heels.

Chapter

5

London, 10 June 2789

'What do we do now?' said Amy, who was steadfastly refusing to look at the corpse. She was stoically maintaining a stiff upper lip, but Rory could tell she was deeply affected by the sight of the woman's body. He knew how she felt.

He was stooped over the body, rummaging in the dead women's pockets, searching for any clues as to what might have happened to her, what might have caused her to perish in such a terrible way. Bleeding out of the eyes like that… he could think of no medical explanation for it. She didn't appear to be wounded in any way, although her clothes had been torn as if she'd been in a fight.

'It's Gradius,' he said a moment later, producing an ID card from the woman's pocket. 'Professor Celestine Gradius.' He stared at the pretty face that smiled back at him from the photograph. 'I was expecting someone... well, you know. Someone more like a...'

'... man?' said Amy. 'Go on, admit it, you were expecting an old man, weren't you? A mad professor, with a wispy grey beard and hairs growing out of his ears.'

'Well, weren't you?'

Amy shrugged. 'I suppose I was,' she sighed, but there was little humour in it. 'I certainly wasn't expecting *this*. I mean... look at the state of her. It's awful.'

'Poor woman,' said Rory, darkly. 'Now we know why the hologram thought there was nobody here. Technically, it was right.'

'Do you think one of her experiments might have gone wrong?' asked Amy. Her expression was serious; all sense of exuberance and joy had long since been dispelled. She looked pale and tired. Rory wished that the Doctor would hurry up.

He shrugged. 'I suppose so,' he said, glancing around the hangar. 'I mean, what else could have caused her to bleed out of her eyes like that?'

He looked back at the body, and then turned away, preferring not to dwell on the sight of the corpse. He'd seen bodies before, in the hospital – of course he had – but that was different. He found it difficult to articulate why. It was something to do with the fact that they were meant to be there. Those people had been ill, or hurt, and they were in a place where they were meant to live or die, the place where that sort of thing was supposed to happen, where decisions like that were made.

Here, in this strange, futuristic workshop, lying in the shadow of a time-travelling ship, the body was just incongruous. Wrong.

At least, he supposed, it hadn't yet started to decompose.

'I think we should try to alert the authorities,' he said. 'We could go to one of those booths, ask for help.'

Amy shook her head. 'I'm not sure that's such a good idea,' she said.

Rory frowned. 'What's wrong? Other than the fact you're standing over the corpse of a scientist from the twenty-eighth century, that is.' He felt immediately foolish for spouting such a flippant comment, but Amy smiled weakly, realising he was only trying to cheer her up.

'Think about it for a minute. We're not from around here. We're trespassing. No one will have any records of our identities. That hologram even told us that Professor Gradius wasn't at home. There must be a system that keeps track of everyone's movements, and it's not going to recognise us. As far as the twenty-eighth century is concerned, we don't exist.'

Rory frowned as he worked her chain of reasoning through to its logical conclusion. 'And the fact we're strangers who found the body while trespassing in her lab might implicate us in her death.'

Amy nodded. 'If there happened to be more to

her death than a botched experiment, well…'

Rory shrugged, getting to his feet. 'Yes. Good point, well made.' He sighed. 'So we wait here for the Doctor, then? Here, with a strange time machine and a corpse. Brilliant.'

Amy nodded again. 'Yes. But we could wait upstairs in reception. The Doctor should be back soon.'

'He's only been gone a few hours.'

'Time travel, remember!' Amy rolled her eyes dramatically.

'Yes, but how's he going to find us?'

Amy waved her hand dismissively and made for the stairs. 'He'll find us. He always does.' She stopped suddenly, her face creasing in concern. 'Hang on. What was *that*?'

'What was what?' said Rory, perplexed.

'Shhh.' She waved him quiet. A second later there was a quiet rapping sound from somewhere beneath their feet.

'*That*,' said Amy, pointedly.

Rory dropped to his knees. 'It sounded as if it was coming from down there,' he said, studying the ground beneath them.

'You don't think these experiments involved drilling, do you? I could do without the earth suddenly opening up beneath my feet again,' said Amy, nervously, stepping back and studying the ground where she'd been standing.

'No,' said Rory, a smile spreading on his face. 'But you've been standing on a trapdoor.' He listened carefully for a minute. There it was again – the same rapping sound, like someone hammering on a door with their knuckles, only far away.

'There's someone down there,' said Amy. 'Someone's trapped down there.' She dropped to her haunches and ran her fingers around the edges of the wide trapdoor, which appeared to be little more than a square cut into the concrete floor of the hangar. 'How do I open this thing? There's no handle.'

Rory shuffled over until he was kneeling beside her. 'Hold on.' He put his hand over hers to stop her for a moment. 'Have you considered that we might not want to let them out?'

Amy glanced at him, confusion in her eyes. 'What?'

'There may be a reason they're down there. What if they're the ones who're responsible for Professor Gradius looking the way she does?'

Amy paused for a moment, and then shook her head. 'No. We'll have to take that risk. We can't leave someone trapped down there, Rory. Innocent until proven guilty and all that.' She returned to running her fingers around the rim of the trapdoor once again, searching for a way to pop it open. 'Gah! If only the Doctor was here with his sonic screwdriver,' she said. 'It must have been sealed with some sort of complex locking mechanism.'

'Have you tried…' Rory leaned over and pushed down on the far right corner of the trapdoor. There was a loud click, and it popped open with a sigh.

'… That?' he finished, sitting back and feeling more than a little smug. He decided it would work out better for him if he decided against rubbing it in.

Amy reached forward and eased the trapdoor back on its hinges, which groaned in protest at the motion. She allowed the door to fold back on itself, striking the ground with a loud bang.

Rory peered into the hole. There was nothing there but a silky puddle of darkness and a cold breeze swirling up from below. He felt a shudder run along the length of his spine. 'Perhaps we were wrong? Perhaps we were hearing things? It might have been the rattle of old pipes, or the so—' He stopped suddenly as a head shot up out of the hole, causing Amy to fall back with a cry and Rory to call out in alarm. He leapt to his feet and scrabbled about on a nearby workbench, looking for anything he could use to defend them with. In the confusion, he grabbed for the nearest tool he could reach and brandished it before him in what he hoped was a threatening manner.

A voice boomed suddenly and urgently out of the head – a deep, male voice with a distinct mechanical edge. 'Do not be alarmed,' it said, and Rory stepped back from the hole, taking a moment to absorb what was happening. His heart was hammering in his chest as if it were trying to burst its way out through his ribcage.

The head was that of an AI – just like the other examples they had seen around the city. Rory watched as it turned to look at them both in turn, and then twisted its neck to survey the rest of the hangar. It blinked, and he was momentarily taken aback by how well the machine was able to mimic the human gesture.

This close, the synthetic nature of the AI's flesh was clearly evident. It was pale, rubbery and didn't vary in tone like a human face. The eyebrows and eyelashes were perfectly shaped and its pate was smooth and unblemished. It looked too perfect to be true, too idealistic to be human. Its eyes, however, looked every bit as human as Rory's own: bright blue and darting frantically from side to side. If anything, it looked *nervous*.

Rory clutched the tool before him like a weapon, hoping he at least looked as if he could defend himself.

'A set square? Seriously?' Amy sounded incredulous, rather than scared. 'Of all the possible weapons in here, you picked a set square?'

He glanced down at the thing in his hand, and then pulled a dejected face. A set square. *Yeah, that was going to help*. He shrugged and waved it threateningly at the AI regardless. 'I could do some damage with a set square,' he said, unconvincingly.

'Have they gone?' said the AI, clearly ignoring him.

'Have who gone?' asked Amy, leaning forward as if studying the machine's face. As far as Rory was concerned, she was getting uncomfortably close to the AI.

'I'll take that as a yes,' it replied. It twisted

suddenly and its left hand shot out of the hole, scrabbling at the ground by Amy's boots, its rubbery fingers scraping on the concrete as it tried to find purchase.

Amy shuffled backwards, avoiding the reach of the spidery fingers. She glanced nervously over at Rory. He thought about rushing forward to stab at the fingers with the set square, but realised that wouldn't help the situation, and Amy was already out of its reach.

After a moment, the hand stilled and the AI turned its gaze on Rory. 'May I request some assistance in extracting myself from this inspection pit?' it said.

'Erm…' said Rory, unsure what to do.

Amy glowered at him and nodded her head in the direction of the AI, her eyes wide with embarrassment. 'Go on,' she mouthed. Then, sighing and shaking her head when he didn't respond, she edged forward and caught hold of the AI's extended arm. She never had been big on subtlety.

'Oh, right. Of course.' Rory stuttered. He dropped the set square and inched forward, reaching gingerly down into the pit as if he expected something to bite him in the darkness. His fingers closed around the AI's other limb. The flesh of its forearm felt cold and pliable, but he could feel the hard skeleton underneath. He decided he really wouldn't want to end up on the wrong side of the machine.

Rory set his feet on either side of the pit and looked over at Amy. 'Ready?'

She nodded.

'One, two, three…'

He heaved with all his strength, staggering backwards as he and Amy tried to drag the artificial man free of the hole. He tumbled over onto his backside a moment later, and Amy fell back with a grunt, leaving the machine slumped half-in and half-out of the hole, its legs still dangling down into the empty void. He let go of its hand and it planted both of its palms firmly on the ground, dragging itself the rest of the way out by itself.

'Whoever… you… are…' said Rory, between gasping breaths, 'you're… heavy…'

The AI clambered to its feet, dusting itself down. It must have been over two metres tall and was dressed in a white shirt – now thick with grime – and black trousers. 'My designation is RVN-73,' it said. 'I am Professor Gradius's assistant. Thank you for your help.'

'RVN-73,' repeated Amy. 'RVN… RVN… Arven!' She beamed at the AI. 'Hello, Arven.'

Rory shook his head, and the AI frowned in apparent confusion. 'Professor Gradius?' it said, its voice solemn.

Amy stopped smiling and shook her head. 'Behind you,' she said. 'I'm afraid she didn't make it.'

Arven – the name was now stuck in Rory's head – turned towards the ship. For the first time Rory saw the great furrows that had been torn into his back, slashing the fabric of his shirt and gouging his rubbery flesh so that the metal skeleton beneath was exposed.

The AI crossed to where the body of Professor Gradius was sprawled on the concrete like a discarded ragdoll. 'Your human forms are so fragile. I tried to help her… to stop them, but they did something to her mind.'

Arven paused for a moment, as if gathering his thoughts. His eyes had taken on a haunted quality. There was an infinite sadness in the look he gave the corpse of his former mistress, and Rory couldn't tell if it was simply respect, or something more. Perhaps the AI was actually capable of feeling human emotions, or at the very least emulating them incredibly well.

'When they realised I was not human they tried to tear me apart,' he went on. 'They were swarming at me from all sides, blocking all of the exits, so I threw myself down into the inspection pit and locked myself inside. It was only later that I realised it couldn't be opened again from within.'

'How long have you been down there?' asked Rory.

'A day, perhaps longer,' said Arven.

'You said they did something to her mind?' said Amy.

Arven nodded. 'The last thing I heard her scream was for them to get out of her head.'

Amy glanced at Rory. 'The Doctor said the Squall were a race of psychic parasites.'

'The Doctor?' said Arven.

'He's… a friend,' said Rory noncommittally.

'So Professor Gradius was running experiments with time-travel technology?' said Amy, pressing on with her questions.

'Yes… but how did you know about that?' Arven looked confused. 'Who exactly are you?'

'I'm Amy and this is Rory. We're… well, it doesn't matter. The important thing is that those experiments are the reason those creatures were here.'

'But the Doctor said the Squall had infected the past,' said Rory.

Amy shrugged. 'And now it looks like they've infected this time period, too,' she said, indicating the corpse on the ground nearby. 'The evidence kind of speaks for itself.'

'So the monsters are here, too, and the Doctor's gone back to 1910 to look for them. Leaving us here. Where there are monsters,' Rory reiterated the word 'monsters' in case Amy had missed it the first time.

There was a clattering sound from behind them. As one, Rory, Amy and Arven turned towards the direction of the sound. Rory gawped at the sight that confronted him.

A strange bipedal creature, so thin it was almost skeletal, stood watching them from the bottom of the stairwell. It had a grey, leathery hide and its beady red eyes regarded them with obvious malice. Membranous flaps of skin hung loose between its elbows and its ribcage like a fleshy cloak, and its upturned snout twitched as it sniffed deliberately at the air. It was tapping the tips of its long, bony fingers menacingly against the metal railings.

As Rory watched, the creature bared its needle-like fangs and hissed at them. To Rory, it sounded almost as if it were a sinister laugh. Behind the creature, the sound of further talons striking the metal treads of the staircase betrayed the fact that it was not alone.

'They're still here,' said Arven, quietly. 'Get behind me.'

'I knew we should have looked upstairs first!' Rory said. He reached down, picked up the set square he'd dropped earlier and threw it at the nearest creature, which squawked angrily as it batted it aside with its arm. It stalked forward, raising its claws.

The hairs on the nape of Rory's neck prickled with fear. There was nowhere to run. The way out was now completely blocked by a gathering mass of the creatures. He could see them swarming down the stairwell, flooding like a deluge into the hangar.

He had to keep Amy safe. He had to *do* something. If these were the creatures responsible for what had happened to the professor, he had to keep them as far away from his wife as possible.

The staircase, though, was the only exit from the hangar. Whichever way he looked at it, they were trapped.

Rory took a deep breath, refusing to take his eyes off the Squall as it crept slowly into the hangar, taking its time as if it knew there was nowhere for them to run. Its talons looked vicious, and he knew he wouldn't be able to defend himself against the creatures for long. Worse, he could feel a pain beginning to blossom inside his head, like a sharp headache, like something was teasing away at his very thoughts, trying to prise them free.

'We. Are. Squall,' the creatures hissed, their voices grating and unnatural. 'And. We. Shall. Feast.'

'In the pit!' Amy bellowed. 'We can hide in the pit!' She started forward, but Arven caught her wrist, swinging her around to face him.

'No. It can't be opened from the inside. If you find yourself trapped down there there'll be no getting out. You'd die without food or water if no one comes.'

'Oh, great,' said Rory, stepping forward and readying himself for the coming attack. 'So it's a choice between starving to death or having our minds sucked out by inter-dimensional parasites.'

'What about in here?' yelled Amy, backing up until her hands encountered the fuselage of the ship. She grimaced as she stepped over the body of the dead professor and peered into the open hatchway. 'Come on!'

'You've got to be kidding!' Rory called to her through gritted teeth. 'We'll be trapped in there, too!' The pain in his head was excruciating and his eyes were beginning to swell, filling with pressure. It was like the worst migraine he'd ever had, a deep, painful throbbing, as if something inside his skull was trying desperately to escape. He issued a low moan of pain, despite himself.

'It's not like we have any other choice!' came Amy's desperate reply.

Without warning, Arven suddenly lurched forward, grabbed Rory by the shoulders and shoved him violently back towards the ship. Rory stumbled and almost fell, catching himself on the edge of the hatchway and tumbling awkwardly inside.

'I'll hold them off,' the AI said, as Amy pulled Rory to safety in the belly of the ship.

The Squall now completely filled the space around the base of the stairwell. There were five, six of them, possibly more, and they were completely blocking the exit. 'There. Is. Nowhere. To. Hide... The. Squall. Shall. Consume. All... The. Hive. Shall. Subsume. This. World... The. Hive. Shall. Manifest... We. SHALL. Feed.'

Rory shook his head, trying to clear the fog of pain and confusion. He could see Amy was now suffering from the same effects, her hands clutching desperately at her head, trying to stave off the flowering pain. Only Arven, the artificial man, seemed immune to the creature's psychic ministrations.

The lead Squall leapt at Arven, spreading its membranous wings and screeching in fury as it buried its talons deep in the rubbery flesh of the AI's chest.

'Arven!' Amy cried, pushing her way to the open hatchway. Rory grabbed her and held her back inside the confines of the ship, trying to prevent her from putting herself in the creature's way.

'We need to shut the door!'

'No! Not without Arven!' she said, clinging on to the lip of the hatchway.

The AI was battling the creature frantically, trying to fend off its rending limbs. With immense strength he grabbed the Squall around the waist and wrenched it free, holding it writhing above his head before slamming it down hard against the concrete floor. It bellowed in fury, flapping a broken arm uselessly as it tried to scramble to its feet.

The remaining Squall, as if on cue, rushed forward en masse, suddenly engulfing the AI.

'Arven!' Amy screamed.

There was no response, other than the screeching of the Squall as they set upon the AI.

Cursing, Amy shook herself free of Rory's grip and threw herself out of the ship into the hangar.

'Amy!' Rory called after her in frustration. 'Amy, get back here!'

Amy ignored him, rushing instead towards the morass of flailing limbs, covering her face in the crook of her arm and reaching out, grabbing hold of the AI's arm as he tried to defend himself against the creatures. Arven twisted around to look at her in surprise, and Rory saw with horror that half of the rubbery flesh that covered his face had been gouged away. It hung in stringy lumps beneath his left eye, exposing the bright steel skeleton beneath.

'Quickly!' Amy cried, admonishing the artificial

man as she tried to drag him back toward the ship. Arven, in response, seemed to fight with renewed vigour, and he wrestled the Squall free, tearing one of them off his shoulder and kicking out at another that was busy attempting to wrench his left leg free from its socket.

Rory was up and out of the ship again now, and he hurried to Amy's side, bustling her back into the hatchway and ducking in behind her, just as another of the Squall leapt up onto Arven's back. The AI twisted and turned, trying desperately to shake the creature free as its wings battered his face and hands.

Arven groaned in frustration as the Squall wrenched another chunk of his rubbery flesh free in its talons. He turned on the spot, slamming himself back against the hull of the ship and crushing the Squall on his back, causing it to momentarily loosen its grip. He took advantage of the brief reprieve, diving headfirst through the open hatchway and almost crushing Rory in the process, who had to leap to one side to avoid being bowled over.

Amy grabbed urgently at the door and slammed it shut, catching one of the creature's wrists in the process as it tried to claw its way inside. It squealed and thrashed at the opening, its hand spasming open and closed, and so Amy raised the door and slammed it shut once again, this time causing the creature to wail and withdraw its damaged limb.

The door clicked shut, and the three of them were plunged into absolute darkness.

They stood for a moment in the belly of the time ship, trying to catch their breath. The only light was the faint glow of Arven's eyes, pale and haunting, twin orbs searching their faces in the gloom. Rory wondered if the AI could actually see in the dark, or whether it could simply sense them there and didn't know where else to look.

'Are you hurt?' asked Amy, her voice tremulous.

'I do not feel pain,' Arven replied, although Rory thought he could hear something – anxiety, perhaps – in the AI's voice. Perhaps the machine didn't feel pain, but it was certainly jumpy.

Outside, the Squall were clawing away at the outer skin of the ship, their claws scratching noisily at the polished metal plating. Others were banging and shaking the vessel as they searched for a means to get inside. Rory felt like a sardine in a can, trapped and waiting for someone to peel back the aluminium lid and snatch him out for dinner. The thought didn't do much to put him at ease.

'Well, I wasn't expecting *that*,' Rory said, with disdain.

Amy gave a nervous laugh and clutched at his arm. 'I hope the Doctor's having more luck,' she said.

He hoped she couldn't feel him trembling. His head was still pounding, and he had the disturbing sensation of something crawling around inside his head, like a spider sifting through his thoughts. He shuddered.

Rory watched Arven's eyes flickering back and

forth as he followed their conversation.

'So this is a time ship, is it?' said Amy, addressing her question at the AI.

'Yes, although it's only an experimental model. It's been tested on short hops of up to a few minutes.'

'It's a lot smaller than the TARDIS,' Rory said, hunched up against the bulkhead to avoid banging his head on the curved roof.

There was a terrifying *clang*, and the whole vessel gave a sudden, violent shudder. 'What the…?' started Rory, but never finished his sentence. There was another bang, and then another. The Squall were clearly striking the outer skin of the ship with whatever tools they could find on the workbenches.

'They're trying to get in,' said Arven. 'They're trying to break in through the hull.'

'Will they do it?' asked Rory.

'With time,' Arven confirmed. 'There are so many of them, and they have such strength…'

'Then we have to work out how to pilot this thing,' Amy said, releasing her grip on Rory's arm. 'We have to use the ship to get out of here. It's our only chance.'

Again, Arven's eyes turned towards her in the darkness. It was an eerie experience, like watching two tiny moons revolving in a sea of black. 'I can pilot this vessel,' he said in his usual monotone.

'Then what are you waiting for?' replied Amy, and her voice was once again filled with her characteristic confidence. 'Take me to 1910, mister RVN-73! The sixteenth of October!'

Arven glanced at Rory, a question in his eyes.

'Better do what she says,' said Rory, grinning. 'I certainly wouldn't want to get on the wrong side of her.'

'Oi!' said Amy, slapping him – playfully – on the arm.

'I must warn you the vessel has not yet been tested with a living occupant,' said Arven. 'The risks are manifold.'

Rory glanced at Amy but couldn't make out her expression in the darkness. Another clanging sound reverberated around the ship as the creatures outside continued with their attempts to smash their way in. He could hear them clambering over the hull, could imagine their fangs glistening in the harsh electric light of the hangar. 'Another five minutes and there won't *be* any living occupants,' he said.

'Besides, we're used to this time travelling stuff…' said Amy nonchalantly.

'Very well,' said Arven, rising to his feet and steadying himself against the bulkhead as the vessel gave another violent rock. A moment later he was gone, worming his way through the narrow space towards the front of the ship.

Rory and Amy remained silent, listening to the scratching of the Squall so close to their heads. 'It'll be OK,' said Rory, but he knew it was more an attempt to convince himself than reassure Amy.

Seconds later, red lights winked on throughout

the ship, casting everything in a disturbing, blood-coloured hue. Rory peered along the spine of the small ship. It was pretty much an empty shell, filled with nothing but trailing wires and banks of switches. Up in the pilot's pit, Arven had strapped himself into a low bucket seat and was busy operating the controls, tapping screens and turning dials. It looked decidedly low-tech for a twenty-eighth-century invention.

Rory turned to Amy who, despite her earlier moment of bravado, was wearing a decidedly worried expression. He reached out and took her hand.

'Here goes nothing,' she said.

Rory offered her a weak smile. 'I wonder if it'll be as hairy a ride as the TARDIS,' he said.

'I wouldn't count on it,' she replied. 'Not without the Doctor at the controls.'

Rory squeezed her hand. 'At least we're together.'

'Hold on!' Arven called back to them. The vessel began to vibrate, shaking violently as if building up a head of steam. Rory grabbed for a loop of overhanging cable, using it to brace himself as the metal shell rattled and bucked. He could hear Squall screeching loudly as they were thrown from their perches.

'Whhhooooaaaaa…' Amy called, squeezing his hand, until the end of her cry was lost in the midst of an almighty clap as the vessel ripped an aperture in the fabric of time and space and slammed itself through into the swirling blue-grey Vortex.

Rory squeezed his eyes shut and held on to Amy for all he was worth.

He hoped the Doctor would be waiting for them at the other end.

Chapter
6

London, 16 October 1910

'Well, Doctor. I must admit that you were right about that miraculous screwdriver of yours. Lucky you thought to keep it with you.' Angelchrist was still trying to catch his breath as he sat in the passenger seat of his own open-topped motor car, barrelling along in the early hours of the morning, searching the skies for any sign of the alien creatures that had been harrying them for the last half an hour.

They had run for what seemed like miles, weaving their way through a warren of dubious alleyways and fog-laden streets, conscious all the while of the creatures baying at their heels. Angelchrist had led the way, adrenalin surging through his veins, calling behind for the Doctor to try to keep up. He'd taken them on a circuitous route, down cobbled streets lined with drunken wastrels freshly spilled out from the public houses, past the misshapen humps of homeless men bundled up in rags against the cold, in circles around a smartly dressed bobby who called out at them to 'Stop right there!' and, having eventually shaken off the pursuing Squall, back to Angelchrist's motor car, which had hove into view out of the fog, eliciting an exclamation of welcome surprise from the Doctor.

Angelchrist, with a resigned sigh, had climbed straight up into the passenger seat, once again allowing the Doctor to take the wheel.

At present, there was no sign of the Squall, but the professor had the sense that the monsters wouldn't have given up that easily, and as he and the Doctor lurched through the fog-bound streets he kept a watchful eye on the grey canopy above, as if expecting one of the creatures to sweep down on them at any moment.

The Doctor was brooding behind the wheel, his brow furrowed in concentration. He seemed unusually subdued, if the scant few hours in which Angelchrist had known him were anything to go by.

Angelchrist kept replaying their encounter with the Squall over and over in his mind. Something about the nature of the creatures, about their apparent intelligence, had disturbed him more than he'd expected. If they'd simply been animals, then perhaps he'd have found it easier. But to discover they were actually sentient, intelligent creatures… Well, that had turned Angelchrist's expectations entirely on their head.

He stared at the road ahead, watching the skeletal limbs of trees come swimming out of the fog as they flitted past. The fog seemed to distort everything, to soften all the harsh lines of the city, to erode the world.

After a while, he turned to the Doctor. 'Why did they talk like that, Doctor? Finishing each other's sentences.'

'It's a sign that their hive is growing in power,' the Doctor shouted over the noise of the wind, gunning the engine and powering them on through the deserted streets. 'It's eerie, isn't it?'

'Yes,' Angelchrist replied with a shudder, but his words were snatched away by the wind. He had no idea what time it was. Late. Or early, he supposed, depending on one's point of view. He realised, with surprise, that he actually had no idea where the Doctor was taking them.

'It's not simply that the Squall are hive creatures,' the Doctor continued, and Angelchrist huddled closer in order to hear. 'Not like wasps or bees. They're far more complex, far more sophisticated than that. They also have a hive mind. They're essentially a single organism with any number of individual bodies or drones. A lone Squall is dangerous, but it's basically a mindless animal, a shell. It exists only to feed the hive, to hunt for prey and gorge itself on their psychic energy.'

The Doctor glanced over to ensure he was following, and Angelchrist nodded for him to continue.

'The hive mind can divide itself between any number of its drones. Each one carries a tiny fragment of the whole. Get more than three of them together and there's enough of it present for it to be able to communicate. Get a horde like the one we saw tonight and you're essentially seeing the individual components of a neural network, all the nodes of a vast and complicated brain.' The Doctor kept his eyes on the road as he talked. Angelchrist got the impression the Doctor was going over it as much for his own benefit as Angelchrist's own, trying to look at the problem from a variety of different angles.

'It's barely credible,' said Angelchrist. He found it hard to conceive of such a bizarre and fascinating race ever evolving into being. And yet here they were, insidiously mounting an invasion of his world.

'When the Squall manifest on a new world, they begin by sending a number of scouts, a handful of drones to investigate. They're essentially parasites, looking for a new energy source to consume. When they find a world rich in psychic power, such as the Earth, they start to increase their numbers. The hive pours more and more of itself through the rift, spreading itself amongst the drones. The more of them there are, the stronger it gets, until eventually the hive mind will have fully manifested on the planet.'

'And then?'

'And then they feast.'

Angelchrist shuddered. That was exactly what

the creatures had said. 'We are Squall, and we shall feast'. At least they were honest about their intentions.

'So that vessel we saw, it was that which caused the Squall to find their way to Earth?'

'The eye of the storm. Yes. That vessel should never have been created.' The Doctor sighed. 'You humans, you're a talented lot. Give you a bunch of tools and you build something. No matter the consequences, no matter the repercussions. You simply have to do it, just because it's there. Put a mountain in front of you and you climb it.' The Doctor beamed at him. 'It's what sets you apart from most of the intelligent life forms out there, professor, out there amongst the stars. You're magnificent. If, perhaps, a little careless sometimes.'

You humans. Angelchrist swallowed. His mouth felt suddenly dry. So that was how the Doctor knew all about the Squall, about the rich and varied universe that existed beyond the confines of the Earth. He wasn't simply from the future, as Angelchrist had assumed. As if that wouldn't have been enough. No, he wasn't even human. And what about his friend, the woman whose pullover he'd found in the claws of the Squall. It was resting on the rear seat now, a puddle of bright red fabric on the dark leather upholstery. Was she an alien, too?

'Doctor? Who's Amy?' Angelchrist cursed beneath his breath for the way he'd simply blurted the question out. He could tell that the Doctor was deeply concerned for her safety.

The Doctor kept his eyes on the road. 'She's a friend,' he said quietly, and Angelchrist decided not to press the matter further.

'What I don't understand is why the army haven't been mobilised? With all these creatures swarming over the city, all these attacks – surely someone must have noticed. Even the police haven't been particularly forthcoming.'

'Ah, that'll be the psychic dampening field,' said the Doctor.

'The what?' replied Angelchrist, bemused.

'The Squall are psychic creatures, professor. They feed on psychic energy, but they also manipulate it. It's how they hunt, suppressing their victim's senses until the last moment, so that they can sneak up on them and pounce.'

Angelchrist shuddered. 'So you mean it's as if they're invisible, right up until the moment they attack?'

'Yes. There could be hundreds – thousands – of them in the city, and people wouldn't even know they were there, at least until it was too late. In fact, the more of them there are, the stronger their abilities become, and the less likely people are to spot them.'

'Then how can *I* see them, Doctor?'

The Doctor grinned over at him, and Angelchrist couldn't help thinking he'd be better off keeping his eyes on the road. 'Well, that's because you're expecting them,' he said, 'Because you have an open mind. You've seen creatures like the Squall before, and you're not afraid to admit they exist. You look at the evidence and don't try to explain it away as something else. Doesn't give the Squall much to work with, you see. They can't play on your ignorance and fears like they can with most people. The majority of the population go about their daily lives without expecting to see monsters lurking in the shadows. So they don't. The Squall make sure of it. But you... you're different, professor. You know about the things that hide in the darkness.'

The Doctor turned his attention back to the road, leaving Angelchrist to ponder his words. *Near-invisible monsters from another dimension.* The very notion was by turns ridiculous and terrifying. And not a little exhilarating. Nevertheless, he was exhausted. He fought to stifle a yawn. 'If you were intending to head back to my laboratory, Doctor, I rather fear we've taken the circuitous route.'

The Doctor grinned again. 'I have a stop to make first, professor. I need to pay a visit to my own ship.'

Angelchrist nodded and leaned back in his seat, pulling his coat more tightly across his chest. It looked as if he was in for a sleepless night. The notion didn't concern him in the slightest.

'I'm sure I left her somewhere around here...' the Doctor mumbled as he strode purposefully through the wispy fog by the river.

'What exactly does this ship of yours look like, Doctor?' asked Angelchrist, trying to keep up. 'Is it similar to the vessel we saw back there at the house?'

'It's a box,' said the Doctor, shaking his head. 'A blue box. A big, blue box.' He smiled affectionately. 'Has the words "Police Box" written on it.'

Angelchrist raised one eyebrow. 'Police?'

The Doctor waved his hand in a dismissive gesture. 'Yes, long story,' he said. 'We'll save that one for another time.' He stopped for a moment, looking thoughtful, and then set off again at a brisk pace. 'Down here,' he said, disappearing down a narrow side street. 'Then down here...' His voice trailed off as he wove his way through the deserted, foggy lanes. Angelchrist followed the sound of his footsteps. 'And then... ah.' The footsteps came to an abrupt halt. There was a moment's pause. 'Um, that's not quite what I was expecting.'

Angelchrist hurried over to join him, turning the corner to find him standing at one end of a long alleyway. 'What is it, Doctor? What have you seen?'

He followed the Doctor's gaze. His question was immediately redundant. At the other end of the alleyway was a tall blue box, just as the Doctor had described. Only, not a great deal of its exterior was visible due to the writhing mass of Squall that were scrabbling all over it, clinging to its surface. There must have been ten or twelve of them, and they seemed entirely oblivious to the Doctor and Angelchrist's presence.

'Fascinating,' said the Doctor. 'It's like they're

drawn to it, swarming all over it as if they can sense the latent time energy. It's like catnip to them, drawing them in like moths to a flame.' He turned to Angelchrist. 'That's the thing about parasites. Always looking for an opportunity, for their next hit. The Squall have spent so long trapped on the other side of reality they've learned to home in on anything that looks as if it might have travelled across dimensions, that carries a certain type of energy signature. The TARDIS is drenched in the stuff. Radiates it. It explains why they were hanging around the time ship, too.'

This was too much for Angelchrist. He had no idea what the Doctor was talking about. He decided to focus on the bit he could fathom. 'What will you do, Doctor? Use your sonic device to shoo them away?' He couldn't help feeling a little nervous in the presence of so many of the creatures. After spending half the night running from them, here they were, facing more of them than ever. He was dog-tired and wasn't sure how much energy he'd be able to muster if it came to that again.

The Doctor shook his head. 'They'll be getting wise to that. There are too many of them. I'll have to try some—' The Doctor gave a brief cry of alarm as something grabbed him from behind and yanked him backwards, causing his sonic screwdriver to rattle away across the cobbles. Angelchrist looked on in horror as he saw that one of the Squall had crept up on them from behind, wrapping its bony, taloned fingers around the Doctor's throat.

The heads of the other Squall in the vicinity – those crawling over the Doctor's ship or lurking at the other end of the alleyway – snapped around in unison, their red eyes glaring in Angelchrist's direction.

The hive mind, thought Angelchrist, glued momentarily to the spot with fear. *It can see me. It's looking at me through their eyes.* He had no idea what to do.

Across the alleyway the Doctor scrabbled at the Squall's hands, trying frantically to prise them free of his throat. The creature squealed in delight, its face a riot of ecstasy as the hive mind began to probe at the edges of the Doctor's psyche.

'You,' it said.

'Shall,' came another voice from somewhere up above them.

'Sustain. Us,' the Squall finished in their bizarre, disjointed tones. 'Your. Mind. Is. Rich… You. Are. Not. Like. The. Others. Of. This. World.'

'No!' The Doctor called between gasping breaths. Angelchrist saw a single tear of dark blood trickle down the Doctor's cheek from the corner of his left eye.

He needed to act. In a moment he knew the other creatures would be upon him. He wouldn't be able to overcome the beasts in hand-to-hand combat; his old bones were simply not strong enough to fend them off. Not in those numbers. He needed to use his brain. What would the Doctor do?

Angelchrist glanced down at the Doctor's sonic

screwdriver resting on the cobbles a few steps away. It was his only hope. Whether they were wise to it or not, he had to give it a try. There was a chance it might buy them enough time to get away.

Taking a deep breath, he dived to the floor, rolling awkwardly and knocking the wind out of himself in the process. He clutched for the sonic screwdriver and kept rolling, just as one of the Squall dropped from the sky, its talons narrowly missing his face.

Twisting over onto his back and holding the sonic aloft like a talisman, Angelchrist pushed one of the buttons, and hoped.

The device emitted its familiar whirring sound, and for a moment nothing happened. Then the Squall all around Angelchrist began to shake their heads violently, screeching in fury and frustration, bashing their temples with their palms as if attempting to dislodge the sound. The beast standing over him fell to its knees with a squawk, and Angelchrist took the opportunity to scramble to his knees, still struggling to regain his breath. He felt lightheaded and wide awake, all sense of his weariness gone.

The Doctor was in the process of extracting himself from his attacker's grasp, pushing it off him as it thrashed about, trying to get away from the sound. It fell to the ground by his feet, writhing and moaning on the cobbles.

'Keep your finger on that button,' said the Doctor, dabbing at his cheek. He looked strangely haunted, and Angelchrist couldn't tell if it was the experience of having his mind invaded by the Squall, or the sight of what his sonic screwdriver was doing to them that concerned him. Angelchrist had never known a man who appeared to be as concerned for the wellbeing of his enemies as he was for his own safety.

'We've got to get out of here,' said the Doctor. 'There are too many of them.'

'What about your ship?'

'The TARDIS will have to wait. Come on!'

Keeping his finger depressed on the button, Angelchrist backed away from the incapacitated Squall, out of the mouth of the alleyway and into the fog-enshrouded street beyond.

Angelchrist placed the tea tray on the table before the Doctor. 'Here, Doctor, a restorative cup of tea. I always find it helps, even in situations such as this.'

The Doctor grinned and reached for the old clay teapot. It was roughly made and etched with a five-pointed star and two short lines of Sanskrit. It was one of Angelchrist's greatest treasures, obtained during an adventure nearly a decade earlier.

'That's the Englishman's answer to everything, isn't it?' said the Doctor, smiling. Angelchrist poured the milk and the Doctor splashed the hot brown liquid into the two teacups. 'A good cup of tea. And you're right, professor. It does seem to make everything a little bit better.'

Angelchrist smiled. 'So what are we going to

do now?' he said, easing back into his chair. He felt decidedly weary, right down to his bones, and his eyelids were growing heavy. Now they were here, back at his laboratory, the events of the night seemed distant already, as if he might have imagined them, as if they might have happened to someone else. Now that he was surrounded by his familiar comforts, safe in his own home, he could barely conceive of the remarkable things he had seen. If it hadn't been for the eccentric figure sitting opposite him, this madman from another world, Angelchrist would have been forced to consider himself quite insane.

'The hive is growing in strength,' said the Doctor, cutting through Angelchrist's reverie. 'It needs to be stopped.'

'But how, Doctor? Even you were no match for them this evening. One man and a screwdriver can only do so much.'

The Doctor smiled, sipping at his tea. 'Oh, I shouldn't worry about that, professor. One man and a screwdriver can achieve more than you think. One man and a screwdriver can save the universe, if he puts his mind to it. Besides,' a broad grin spread over his face, 'I've got you to keep an eye out for me.' He placed his teacup pointedly on the table between them. 'Now, before we proceed I've got something terribly important to ask you.'

'Yes, Doctor? Anything.' Angelchrist leaned forward in anticipation.

'Do you have any custard creams?' said the

Doctor, clapping his hands together, loudly. 'Tea, I think, is always so much better with a custard cream.'

Angelchrist couldn't prevent himself from breaking into a long, guffawing laugh.

The Doctor offered him a bemused smile, as if he wasn't quite sure of the joke. 'OK...' he said. 'So no custard creams. But I could have a use for a few of the bits and bobs you have lying around here.' The Doctor glanced over at the workbenches and bookcases overflowing with mechanical contraptions, wooden dolls, baubles, trinkets and other assorted oddments. 'A few components here and there.'

'Whatever you need, Doctor. Help yourself.'

'Good man!' the Doctor exclaimed, jumping energetically to his feet. He used his arm to sweep a stack of papers off the table and onto the floor, clearing a space. Angelchrist tried to ignore the mess. 'This is going to take me a while, I'm afraid,' the Doctor said, and then turned and disappeared behind the heaps of boxes at the other end of the lab. Angelchrist heard sounds of him rummaging about amongst the components and equipment there.

He must have dozed off, because the next thing Angelchrist knew there was sunlight streaming in through the window and the Doctor – now in his shirtsleeves – was pouring him a fresh cup of tea. 'Ah, hello!'

Angelchrist blinked at him, bleary-eyed. 'Oh, forgive me, Doctor,' he said sheepishly, rubbing the back of his aching neck and sitting forward, trying to regain his bearings. 'I must have nodded off.'

The Doctor smiled and passed him a china teacup. There was a contraption, of sorts, resting on the table. It was about the size of a man's head and had clearly been assembled from a bizarre assortment of discarded mechanical parts and copper wire. Angelchrist had no notion of what it could be, but it didn't look terribly professional. Whatever the Doctor was, he didn't appear to be a particularly capable engineer.

The Doctor picked up the device, hefting it in hands. He was wearing a broad grin and seemed inordinately pleased with himself. 'It's not the most aesthetically pleasing object,' he said, 'but given the circumstances, I think it's rather beautiful. Even if I do say so myself.'

Angelchrist nearly spluttered on his tea. Beautiful wasn't quite the word he might have used to describe it. 'What is it?'

'An amplifier!' the Doctor said, animated. 'It boosts the range and signal of the sonic screwdriver. Should help to keep those pesky Squall at bay so I can get to the TARDIS. At least for a while, anyway.'

Angelchrist nodded. 'Why is it you need to get to your ship?'

'The instruments in the TARDIS will give me a better idea of the extent of the problem, the size of the rift,' said the Doctor. 'From there I'll be able to work out how to close it. First, though, there's something else we have to do.'

'Breakfast?'

The Doctor shook his head. 'No. Far more important than that. There were no bodies in the wreckage of that time ship. Just a torn red jumper.'

Angelchrist set his empty teacup down on the arm of his chair. 'Surely that's good, isn't it? It suggests they got away from the Squall?'

'Precisely. That's very good. It's very good indeed.'

'So…?' Angelchrist pressed.

'It means only one thing, professor. It means that Amy and Rory are here somewhere, in 1910, and that they're in very grave danger.'

'But how are we going to find them?' said Angelchrist, his brow creased with a heavy frown. 'We don't even know where to begin our search. They could be anywhere.'

'Oh, that's easy,' said the Doctor with an impish grin. 'Whenever you want to find Amy Pond, you simply look for trouble.'

Chapter
7

London, 13 October 1910

Everything was black.

Rory shook his head to clear the grogginess and tried to peel open his eyes. After a moment, he realised they were, actually, open, and he was simply lying in a darkened room.

Lying?

He stirred, feeling the press of cold metal against his right cheek. His left arm was trapped beneath something heavy. He gave it a tug and the thing moved. His head was pounding.

The thing that had been resting on his arm gave a familiar-sounding sigh. Rory blinked, trying to bring himself round. Where had he heard that sound before? That was like... just like... Amy!

He dragged himself up into a sitting position and immediately wished he hadn't. The world swam in wide circles all around him. He had no sense of where he was, or what he'd been doing, not helped by the utter, impenetrable darkness. He had the vague sense that he'd been in a workshop or laboratory, but everything was fuzzy and distant. Where was the Doctor?

Suddenly, his memories began to snap into focus. London. The river. Professor Gradius, the AI, the Squall, the time ship... Ah. The time ship.

Rory ran a hand through his hair. Well, at least they were still alive. He heard Amy give a low groan and reached out for her. His hand touched something soft.

'Oi! Get your hand out of my face.'

So, Amy was all right, then. That was good. That was very good. 'Are you OK?' Rory croaked, feeling the need to ask her regardless.

'I will be when you move your legs,' she replied.

Rory frowned. What did she mean? He shifted around, causing Amy to yelp and realising that, at some point during the landing – if, indeed, they *had* landed – they must have been bowled over and become somehow entwined.

'Sorry,' he said, extracting himself and feeling around in the darkness for something to hold on to.

Amy laughed. 'I was grateful for the soft landing,' she said.

Rory rubbed his head. He gathered he must have struck it as he'd fallen. Either that or the probing of the Squall had done more damage than he'd imagined. 'Have we stopped moving?' he asked.

'A couple of minutes ago,' said Amy. 'I've been trying to wake you.' So that was why his other cheek was stinging.

'Arven?' he asked.

'I don't know,' said Amy, her voice level. He sensed her shifting about, climbing to her feet in the confined space.

Grasping hold of a bundle of loose cables, Rory hauled himself up. He was still feeling dizzy and disorientated, but the spinning had stopped, and his eyes were finally beginning to adjust to the gloom. It was dark, but he could just about make out his surroundings. He took a couple of steps toward what he thought was the front of the ship, but realised, in the chaos, that he'd completely lost his bearings. He didn't even know which way was up or down.

'Arven?' he called. 'Are you there, Arven?'

'I'm here,' came the reply.

Rory followed the voice, picking his way through the ship, keeping his head bowed to avoid striking it against the low curve of the hull. A moment later he pushed his way through to the pilot's pit, brushing aside an access panel that had come loose during the turbulent journey through the vortex. There was a dull glow in here from a red bulb set into the ceiling. He could see Arven slumped in the pilot's chair.

'Can you switch the lights back on?' said

Rory, struggling his way through a curtain of trailing cables. He could hear Amy moving about behind him, following him through the morass of overhanging wires.

'No,' came Arven's monotone reply. 'Half the control panel is missing. We'll have to make do with what's left of the emergency lighting.'

'Missing?' said Rory. 'As in, we lost part of the ship as we landed?'

'It's more complicated than that,' said Arven. 'The ship doesn't "land" in any conventional sense. It just... appears. It materialises back into reality, phasing back into being at the designated location.'

'Just like the TARDIS,' said Amy, her voice closer now.

'So what went wrong?' asked Rory, unsure exactly where this was leading.

'We materialised in a wall,' said Arven. 'Part of the control panel is buried inside it. So is my arm.' There wasn't even the slightest hint of emotion from the AI, as he calmly delivered this – frankly alarming – piece of information.

Rory stumbled forward in the half-light, trying to make out the shape of the control panel. He almost started in surprise when he realised the space where it ought to have been was occupied instead by a solid brick wall. He reached out and, right enough, his fingers encountered cool, rough brickwork. It seemed as if the wall cut through the entire front end of the vessel. He stepped back, unsure what to say or do next.

'I need your help to disconnect my arm,' said Arven, as if sensing his hesitation. 'It's buried up to the elbow. If we remove it at the shoulder socket I'll be able to get free.'

'Remove your arm!' said Amy, putting a hand on Rory's shoulder in the gloom. 'Bit drastic, isn't it? Can't we just dematerialise the ship and free your arm that way?'

Arven shook his head, twisting around in his seat to look at her.

'I'm afraid it's not that simple,' he said. 'My arm – and the nose of the ship – is now irreversibly bonded with the wall. Assuming there's enough of the ship's circuitry left to dematerialise, we'd end up taking half the wall with us.'

'I bet the Doctor could do it,' said Rory. 'We could leave you here, go and fetch help.'

'Too dangerous,' said Arven. 'Those creatures... the Squall. If they come for me while you're gone they'll tear me apart. I'll have no means of getting away.' He shifted slightly in his seat. 'Please, help me to disconnect my arm. I cannot feel pain. There is no need to be alarmed.'

Rory sighed. To his mind, there was *every* reason to be alarmed. They were stuck inside an experimental time vessel, buried halfway in a wall, with an AI that wanted them to tear off its arm. They had no idea where the Doctor was and whether they'd even successfully managed to make it to 1910. And even if they had made it to 1910, they had no idea where to begin searching for the Doctor, and the place was probably swarming with aliens who wanted to suck out their minds.

Just another day in the life of Rory Williams.

'OK, Arven. We'll help,' said Rory, and he felt Amy squeeze his arm reassuringly. 'You'll have to guide us through it, though. I might be a nurse but I've never done an amputation.'

'Very well,' said Arven. 'Is there room for you to come around the other side of my chair?'

'Yes, I think I can do that,' said Rory. He manoeuvred around to the other side of the AI, squeezing himself in between the edge of the control panel and the chair. He glanced down at where Arven's arm disappeared abruptly into the wall.

It was utterly bizarre. Where the rubbery flesh met the brickwork it seemed to meld seamlessly, merging into one. It wasn't as if the wall had been built around the arm, nor that the arm had somehow been pushed violently inside the wall, becoming trapped. The join was smooth and seamless, and it felt more as if the arm had somehow grown out of the solid brickwork, becoming part of the fabric of the building.

Rory put his hand on Arven's shoulder. 'OK. What do you need me to do?'

'Right, the first thing you need to do is tear away the clothing,' said Arven. 'Then you need to cut away the flesh.'

Rory grimaced, and then remembered that the AI could see his expression. He tried to compose himself. He grabbed a fistful of the AI's shirt and tugged. The garment had already been practically shredded by the Squall, and after a couple of attempts it gave way at the seams, rending free with a loud tear.

'The flesh there is already damaged. Work your fingers into one of the gashes and tear it away.'

Closing his eyes, Rory felt across the rubbery surface of the AI's shoulder until his fingers encountered a wide furrow, caused by the rending talons of the Squall. He worked his fingers into the space until he could feel the metal skeleton underneath. He'd expected it to feel damp and warm, reminiscent of a human body, but instead it felt cold and mechanical, more like a machine than a person. That helped.

'Good. Now strip it away so you can access the metal frame beneath.'

Rory did as Arven asked, pulling away gobbets of the rubbery flesh until the shoulder joint was exposed.

'OK,' he said, dropping the last of it to the floor and telling himself that he didn't feel queasy at all. 'I think we're done.'

He glanced over at Amy, who was close by, watching with interest. 'Good job you had all that medical training,' she said.

'I hardly think it prepared me for amputating the arm of an artificial man,' said Rory, exasperated.

'Now,' Arven said, twisting around to face Rory. 'This is the difficult bit. There's a release mechanism at the base of my neck. You need to find it, depress it, and then twist my arm counterclockwise out of the socket.'

'But your arm is buried in the wall,' he said. 'We'll never get the leverage.'

Arven nodded. 'We will. I'll twist one way while you twist the other.'

Rory felt around the back of Arven's neck until he located the release switch. It was firm and unyielding. 'Are you ready?' he asked.

'Yes,' came the reply.

'Then one, two, three…' Rory tugged on the shoulder joint, twisting it around as firmly as he could. He felt Arven pulling in the opposite direction, trying to give them enough movement to wrench the limb out of its socket.

For a moment they remained locked in that bizarre position, Rory grunting with the effort of maintaining the pressure, Arven twisting around in his seat, working to free his trapped limb from his torso. But then Rory felt something click deep inside Arven's shoulder and a second later the arm popped free, causing the AI to tumble ungracefully to the floor with a loud clatter.

Rory, stunned to be holding the wrong end of someone's arm in his hands – regardless of whether it was artificial or not – stepped back, banging his head painfully against the curved hull of the ship. 'Ow!' he called.

'Are you all right?' asked Amy.

'Yeah,' he said. 'Just a little knock.'

'Not you!' she said. 'Arven!'

The AI was picking himself up off the ground. 'I am quite well,' he said. 'Thank you.'

'You're welcome,' said Rory, although he had no idea to whom the appreciation had been addressed.

'Let's get out of here,' said Amy. 'We need to find the Doctor.'

'Best idea I've heard since "Let's take a trip to the Rambalian Cluster",' said Rory, with feeling.

They snaked their way back through the belly of the time ship, a one-armed Arven leading the way. Within a few moments he had cracked the hatch, which opened with a deep, pneumatic sigh, and then they were peering out into the dusky evening beyond.

'Well, it certainly looks like 1910,' said Rory, contemplatively. He could see they were in the backyard of a terraced Victorian house. It was late and night was beginning to close in. Wispy trails of fog clung to the streetlamps and the moon was already bright and hanging low in the sky.

'It looks like 2010, too,' said Amy. 'I don't suppose these back streets of London change all that much. We need to ask somebody.'

Rory glanced over at Arven, who was standing by the hatchway, looking out over the scene outside. He lowered his voice. 'Asking someone might be a bit difficult, what with the one-armed robot from the far future, here.'

Amy smiled and her eyes sparkled. 'That's what I love about you, Rory Williams. Ever the optimist.'

She grabbed hold of the edges of the hatchway and heaved herself out. As she did so, the sleeve of her red hoody caught on the buckled frame and there was a loud, rending tear of fabric.

'Oh, pants!' she exclaimed, turning to look at the damage. The whole right side of the garment was shredded, hanging loose off her shoulder. Sighing, she pulled it up and over her head, tossing it back inside the ship. Underneath she was wearing a plain black T-shirt. She put her hand out to Rory. 'Jacket,' she said. It wasn't a request.

Rory shrugged off his coat and handed it to her. She smiled sweetly and slipped it on. He clambered out of the ship to stand beside her, his feet sinking into the soft loam of a flattened flowerbed. The air out here smelled as if there'd just been a thunderstorm, fresh and sharp. Rory could hear voices coming from the neighbouring yard and lights had blinked on in some of the windows further along the street.

'Er, I think our arrival might have drawn some attention,' said Rory, looking up and down the row of terraced houses. When Amy didn't reply, he nudged her, trying to get her attention. 'Amy?'

Wordlessly, she tugged on his sleeve. He turned to see what the problem was.

Standing across the yard, no more than three metres away, was a slavering, chittering Squall. It blinked at them as if it were a little disorientated, but nevertheless bared its fangs in apparent warning. Behind the creature the air shimmered gently, as if in a heat haze, and Rory had the sense that something terrible was about to happen.

'They're coming,' he said, taking Amy by the hand and walking her slowly backwards from the ship. Arven followed suit, keeping his eyes on the lone alien. 'In a moment we're going to have to run. We're going to have to get out of here as quickly as we can.'

'What are you talking about?' said Amy. 'What's coming?'

'They are,' said Rory, pointing to the shimmering haze just as a hundred grey-skinned limbs burst through it at once, the sky suddenly filling with Squall as more and more of them poured through the dimensional rift. They swarmed over the wreckage of the ship, swung up onto the window ledges of the nearby houses and glided over the rooftops, eliciting cries of terror from the people who had come out into their gardens to find out what the noise of the crashing ship had been about. Their cries soon turned to wails of horror as the Squall descended, setting about their grisly psychic feast.

Amy and Rory turned to face one another. Amy looked terrified, and Rory could only imagine the expression on his own face. They'd travelled a thousand years into the past to escape the monsters, and now here they were, still threatening to consume their minds, or worse. He'd expected at least a few hours' respite before the Doctor found them and dragged them back into the whole sorry mess. It seemed that wasn't to be.

'Run!' they cried in unison, fleeing up the garden

path and bursting through the back gate into the stench-filled alleyway beyond. Arven barrelled along after them, keeping his head down as he ran.

They shot out onto a busy street a moment later, skidding to a halt as they tried to decide which way to run. The people around them seemed utterly oblivious, bustling along minding their own business, returning home after a long day's work or an evening in the pub. Primitive motor cars nudged horses out of the way on the road, their drivers trundling along without any heed of the pedestrians or other road users. One woman screamed when she caught sight of Arven, his artificial flesh hanging in loose tatters from his metal face, and Rory quickly ushered him on, keeping to the shadows, trying to put as much distance between them and the Squall as possible.

He had no idea if the creatures had given chase, but he dared not look back, dared not think about what might happen if the Squall caught up with them, focusing only on getting them to safety as swiftly as he could. The thought of the poor people who'd already fallen to their clutches filled him with a hollow feeling, a sharp pang of guilt, even though he knew there had been nothing they could have done.

They ran for ten or fifteen minutes, until Rory's chest was burning and his feet hurting from the constant, relentless pounding. He slowed, coming to rest by the low wall of a churchyard to catch his breath.

Behind him, the church loomed out of the gloom; a bleak, gothic structure decorated with all manner of ostentations, crenellations and gargoylish faces. Around it, the listing headstones of the graveyard looked like a forest of broken teeth in the gloaming. Fog curled around them like smoky fingers, reaching out from beyond the grave to snatch at the ankles of the living. Rory shivered at the thought. Clearly, he'd been watching too many horror films.

He glanced up at Amy as she dropped onto the wall beside him. 'Do you think they followed us?' she said.

'I doubt it,' he replied through gasping breaths, shaking his head. 'Too many people.' He glanced up at the sky, just to be sure. None of the creatures – he was pleased to see – were circling overhead.

Arven was standing nearby, probing the socket where his arm used to be.

Amy held out a newspaper.

'Where did you get that from?' asked Rory.

'From a stand back there. Picked it up as we ran past.'

'You mean you stole it?'

'More like… borrowed it,' she said, smiling. 'Well, it's not like I had any old pennies to pay for it.'

'I suppose not,' said Rory. He took it from her and unfolded the front page. 'Oh,' he said.

'*Oh*, what?' said Amy. 'That sounded ominous.'

'*Oh*, nothing,' said Rory, folding the paper away again and putting it behind his back. '*Oh*, you don't have to worry.'

Amy narrowed her eyes. 'Give me that newspaper!'

'We don't have time for this now, Amy.'

'Give it to me,' she said reprovingly. 'It's *my* newspaper!'

'Well, technically not, since you *borrowed* it.'

She reached around his back and wrestled it out of his hands. 'Um, you might not want to do that. Not now.'

Amy gave him *the look*, and unfolded the front page on her knee. He waited while she scanned the dateline. 'The thirteenth of October 1910! We're three days early!'

Arven look up from the ruins of his shoulder. 'I told you, it's an experimental ship. Three days is good. Three days is lucky. We could have been off by *years*.'

'And let's face it, Amy – we've both waited much longer before,' said Rory with a shrug. 'Three days isn't going to kill us.'

'No. But *they* might,' said Amy, an expression of sudden alarm on her face. Rory twisted around to see three Squall picking their way between the headstones toward them, their eyes blazing with menace.

'Quickly, into the church,' said Arven.

'Something tells me that religion isn't going to stop them,' said Rory.

'Perhaps not,' said Arven. 'But thick wooden doors just might.'

'Excellent point,' said Amy. She turned to Rory,

indicating the AI with a nod of her head. 'He's good at this.'

'Go on! Get in there after him,' said Rory, leaping over the wall and squelching across the muddy loam toward the entrance.

Behind them, the three Squall hissed in unison. 'We. Are. Squall. And. We. Shall. Feast.'

Chapter
8

London, 13 October 1910

The church was cold and empty. Their footsteps echoed in the cavernous space as Rory, Amy and Arven hastily took cover inside.

'Help me with this,' said Arven, attempting to close the heavy oak doors with his remaining arm. Rory ran to his aid, pushing them shut and sliding the deadbolts into place. Within seconds, the doors were bucking violently in their housing as the three Squall threw themselves against the other side, trying to force their way in.

'Great. Now we're trapped again,' said Amy, despondently.

Rory looked around, trying to get his bearings. The building was ancient and sombre, solidly built, thick stone walls inset with rows of stained glass windows. The sunlight shining through them cast colourful patterns over the rough wooden furniture below.

'They're not going to give up,' said Arven, and as if to underline his point there was a tremendous bang from above as the creatures tried to batter their way in through the roof. Rory saw dark shadows flitting past the windows.

'There's more of them,' he said. 'They've found us.'

'It won't take them long to work out they can break in through the windows,' said Amy. 'We need to think of a plan.'

'We can barricade the doors with some of those pews,' said Rory, pointing at the ranks of wooden benches lined up behind them.

'They'll still be able to get in through the windows,' said Arven. 'Amy's right. We don't have very long.'

Amy crossed to the altar at the far end of the hall. 'Do you think there's another way out?' she called, her voice echoing around them.

Rory shrugged. 'Probably. But that won't do us much good. They'll be waiting outside.'

'No, I don't mean a back door,' said Amy. 'These old churches always have hidden nooks and crannies, secret passageways and stuff. You know the sort of thing: dark, dingy tunnels, dead people.'

'I think you've been watching too many horror films,' said Rory. 'But we're running out of options.' He went to join Amy. Behind him, the Squall were scratching frantically at the doors with their talons. He could hear hordes of them chittering and squawking outside.

'OK,' he said, determinedly. 'There's got to be something around here. Some other way out. Arven, can you keep an eye on those Squall while Amy and I take a look around?'

The AI nodded and turned to face the door. Rory turned to tell Amy they should split up, but found she'd already gone. Sighing, he set out after her.

Behind the altar and pulpit was a series of smaller rooms – private rooms, Rory assumed – for the vicar. They were sparsely furnished. One of them contained only a beaten old table and a few chairs, along with a basic stove and tea-making equipment. Another held a desk and a number of bookcases, the shelves lined with row-upon-row of musty leather-bound tomes. The doors were solid enough, and if it came to it they'd be able to retreat into one of the rooms, effectively shutting themselves off from the invading Squall, but Rory knew they wouldn't be able to hold out for long.

'Over here!' he heard Amy cry a moment later. He ducked out of the study, picking his way along the narrow stone passageway. He found her standing between two large marble tombs, each of them bearing the solemn-faced effigy of the dead person it contained. She had a triumphant smile on her face.

'See! I told you! A secret passageway.' She stepped to one side, indicating a small doorway behind her. The door was hanging ajar, and Rory saw that it opened onto a flight of worn stone steps. He inched forward and peered into the inky darkness below.

'We can't go down there,' he said. 'It could be anything. A dungeon. A tomb. A dead end.'

'Well it's not like we have any better options,' said Amy pointedly.

Just then, there was a cry from the other end of the church, and their eyes met in concern. 'Arven!' said Rory, turning around and starting back down the passageway. He stopped when he heard Arven's footsteps thundering against the flagstones, heading in their direction.

A second later the artificial man was sliding to a stop before him. 'They're here!' he said urgently. 'They're inside.' Rory could hear them bashing their way in through the priceless windows.

'Secret tunnel it is!' said Amy, reaching through the doorway and yanking something free from a bracket on the wall. It was a wooden torch – an actual, traditional torch – of the sort used to ward off monsters in those same horror films that Rory had joked about with Amy.

'Here, hand me those matches,' said Amy, pointing to a small table covered in altar candles. Rory reached over and retrieved the matchbook from where it lay amongst the white pillars of wax. He pulled a match free, struck it, and put the flame to the proffered torch. It went up with a sudden *whoosh* and, before he knew it, the three of them were descending the steps into the darkness, Amy leading the way, the torch held high above her head.

Rory pushed the door shut behind them. 'No one's been down here for years,' he said, dismayed, as he fought to brush the cobwebs away from his face. They were in some sort of catacomb, a roughly hewn tunnel that was only just high enough for Rory to be able to stand at his full height. Arven, on the other hand, had to stoop to be able to manoeuvre in the confined space.

Innumerable alcoves had been carved into the walls, each one occupied by the remnants of the long dead. Some of them bore wooden coffins – or what remained of them – while in others there were simply heaps of dusty bones, wrapped in the occasional rag. The hollow sockets of the skulls seemed to stare at them as they crept along, winding their way further beneath the ancient building.

'These tunnels must go right under the graveyard,' said Amy, using the torch to singe away a particularly dense cluster of spider webs blocking their route. It was an eerie thought to consider they were entirely surrounded by the dead, both in the walls and high above them in the soft ground of the graveyard. Rory suppressed a shudder.

They pressed on like this for some time, mostly in silence, each of them expecting to hear the sounds of the pursuing Squall in the tunnel behind them at any moment. Amy led them along the narrow tunnel as it snaked further and further beneath the city, glancing back every few minutes to check that Rory hadn't fallen behind.

Presently, after what seemed like hours of

trudging through the creepy passageway, Rory became aware of the sound of running water up ahead.

'Urgh!' said Amy in disgust. 'What's that smell?'

'Human waste,' replied Arven in his usual monotone. 'I think we must be nearing the sewers.'

'Sewers?' said Amy. 'Perhaps we should turn back?'

Rory covered his nose and mouth with his cupped hands in an effort to stifle the acrid stench. 'No,' he called. 'No, there'll be a way out through the sewers. If these tunnels meet up with them we'll be able to find a manhole to the street above. There's nothing but Squall back there in the church.' They continued on, slowly growing used to the disgusting scent.

Sure enough, the tunnel soon came to a T-junction that opened out into a dank, brick-built sewer. The walls curved up around them, and filthy water sluiced along in a wide channel, carrying with it all manner of disgusting waste. Rory tried not to look at it.

The writhing forms of rodents scampered out of their way as they edged cautiously along the walkway. 'Rats!' said Amy, with barely concealed horror. 'God, I *hate* rats!' She waved the torch at the sea of them around her boots, and they squealed and shot away, splashing into the water.

'There's a ladder up ahead,' said Arven, pointing to a spot a little further along the tunnel. Rory could just make it out in the semi-darkness, an iron ladder leading up to a manhole high above.

'Come on!' said Rory, urging them forward. 'We'll be out of here in a few minutes.' He took the torch from Amy and squeezed past her, leading them on with renewed vigour.

'Right, you first, Arven,' he said as they came to the foot of the ladder a few moments later. The AI mounted the first rung and began the steady climb to the surface, bracing himself with his legs as he pulled himself up with his one remaining arm. 'Now you, Amy.' He watched until she was safely halfway up the ladder. Then, ditching the torch on the walkway, he followed behind the others.

When he finally got to the top of the ladder, Rory found Arven had already shifted the cover to one side and was hauling Amy out into the street. Rory pulled himself up and out with a loud groan of exertion, and Amy helped him to his feet. He dusted himself down, blinking into the bright sunlight. A small crowd of people were milling around, staring at the three of them in astonishment as Arven slid the manhole cover back into place with a loud *clang*.

'Erm, hello,' said Rory, offering them a little wave. 'Sewer inspection.'

'Yes, and everything's fine,' said Amy, as if that was the end of the matter. 'Ten out of ten.' She grabbed Rory's arm. 'Come *on*!' she said, urgently, and together the three of them, looking somewhat incongruous in their modern clothes, set off at a run, hoping to put as much distance between themselves and the Squall as possible.

*

Three days.

Three days they'd been on the run, moving from location to location, each time hoping they'd happened upon a place where the Squall wouldn't be able to find them, each time being forced to move on when they did.

They'd been constantly on the move, resting for only a few hours at a time, moving around the city, living hand to mouth. They'd managed to purloin some clothes from a washing line in a deserted garden, a long black coat to cover Amy's short skirt, which had already drawn rather too much attention as they'd hurtled through the streets, and a shirt and cap for Arven, the latter of which they'd pulled down low over his face, making it easier for him to hide what was left of his damaged flesh.

They'd eaten only scraps of stolen food, or whatever they'd been able to beg from the scant few people who'd helped them. Arven, of course, needed neither food nor sleep and had proved a constant companion, remaining watchful and alert, keeping an eye on Rory and Amy while they slept.

Wherever they went, however, whatever they tried to do, they seemed unable to shake the constant hounding of the Squall. It was as if the aliens were somehow drawn to them, as if the creatures had picked up their scent and were doggedly refusing to let it go.

Rory suspected there was more to the creature's persistence than the simple impulse to hunt, of course, but he had no way of telling, and no real time to consider it. They hadn't been able to remain in one place for long enough. At one point they'd taken shelter in a house in Kensington – a huge, well-appointed townhouse that appeared to be empty – only to find the still-warm corpse of a burglar laid out on the kitchen floor, surrounded by the scattered spoils of his trade. He'd bled profusely from his eyes, and at the sound of movement from upstairs they had fled again, realising the Squall were already there, waiting for them. They'd spent the night beneath a railway bridge instead, huddled against the cold, wishing they'd been able to find somewhere warm and dry.

The previous day – 16 October – they'd waited with baited breath, waited for the Doctor to come storming out of the misty London morning to find them. Waited for the distant, elephantine roar of the TARDIS's engines. In the end, however, neither had come. The Doctor was somewhere in London, but the likelihood was that he didn't have even the slightest notion that Amy and Rory were there, too.

They'd discussed going back to the scene of the crash, to see if they might find the Doctor poking around in the remnants of the time ship, but the presence of the Squall made that impossible. They knew they'd never even get near the ship, what with the sheer number of creatures in the vicinity.

They'd seen the newspapers too, of course, and were aware of the reign of terror under which the Squall held the city. There had been so many deaths, so many victims. The Squall were all over

London now, picking their victims indiscriminately, plucking them openly from the streets. They loitered in the mouths of dark alleyways, hid around corners or swept down on people from the rooftops, gliding on their translucent wings. The evidence was there before everyone's eyes, but the police seemed entirely unable to acknowledge it, attributing the deaths to the work of an imaginary serial killer.

Rory had considered going to them, showing them the evidence himself, but he knew he'd simply be branded a madman and thrown in a cell, or worse, in a sanatorium. That would be no use to anyone, least of all Amy and the Doctor.

Sighing, Rory peeled open his eyes.

Day was breaking. The sunlight slanting in through the window picked out the dust motes ebbing on the stirring currents. He watched them dance for a moment, transfixed.

Amy was still dozing on the pile of woollen blankets beside him, her hair like a spill of bright red ink on the makeshift pillow. Rory decided to let her sleep for a little while longer. He knew that she didn't really need protecting – if anyone could look after themselves, Amy Pond could – but it didn't prevent him from trying. It didn't change anything. He was her husband, and he had a job to do. Keeping her safe was his first priority.

The house they were in had clearly been abandoned for some months, if not longer. It was in a grave state of disrepair. It stank of mildew and damp, and the ceilings had collapsed in a number of places, opening up ragged holes that allowed them to see through to the floor above. They'd decided to remain downstairs for the duration of their brief stay, both to make it easier if they needed to get out in a hurry and to avoid any of them accidentally falling through the rotten floor from above.

They'd found the place almost by accident while trying to lose themselves in the slums of the Whitechapel district, hoping the sheer volume of people, coupled with the stench of the place, would help to throw the Squall off their scent. Rory had been appalled by the things they had seen while wandering the streets, the sheer poverty on display at every turn. The people there lived in absolute squalor, eking out a miserable existence with little or no prospects of ever finding a way out.

It was like something he might expect to see in the Dark Ages. But this – this was the twentieth century. Surely there was no need for people to live like that in 1910.

Whatever the case, he'd been grateful for the empty house they'd discovered here, boarded up down a narrow lane. His survival instincts had kicked in, and together he and Arven had affected a makeshift entrance through a back window. They'd holed up in there for the night, wrapping up against the cold in whatever rags they could find. Now, it was nearly time to move on again. He wondered if today they might find the Doctor. Or rather, if the Doctor might find them.

He felt Amy stirring beside him. She blinked up

at him with sleepy eyes. 'Oh, it's not time to get up already, is it? It's so cold, and I'm so warm in here.'

Rory shrugged. 'I'm afraid so,' he said. 'We've got to get moving before the Squall find us. And besides, today's the seventeenth of October.' He glanced over at Arven pointedly.

'Oh,' said Amy, her mood suddenly changing. She sat up, propping herself on one elbow. They both knew what that meant. The AI they'd seen dredged from the Thames, a thousand years in the future, had been just like Arven. That one had also been missing an arm. It had been in the water for over a thousand years, and it had fallen into the water – the Doctor had said – on 17 October 1910.

It was only a matter of time before Arven found himself in the river. It was practically inevitable, and it was going to happen today.

'I can hardly look at him,' said Rory, in hushed tones. 'I didn't think he'd be like this, so much like a… *person*. I thought he would just be a robot, a tool created for a specific role.'

'I know,' said Amy, putting her hand on his arm. 'But all we can do is try to prevent it from happening.' She sighed. 'I wish the Doctor would hurry up.'

'I've been thinking about that,' said Rory. 'Do you remember in the future, on the embankment, when the Doctor spoke to the AI?'

'Of course.'

'Well, it clearly knew him. It recognised him. And that means that at some point today, before he has his… *accident*, Arven is going to meet the Doctor.'

Amy's eyes widened as the implications of his words struck home. Her face split into a wide grin. 'Oh, you're not just a pretty face, are you?' she said, leaning forward to kiss him brightly on the cheek.

'Now all we have to do is stay alive long enough to find him,' said Rory drily.

'Oh, go on, spoil the moment,' said Amy, but she was smiling.

'Right. Time to get up.' Rory heaved himself up and crossed to where Arven was standing, sentry-like, by the window. 'Morning,' he said. His mouth felt dry as he stood beside the proud figure of the AI. He didn't know what else to say to it, couldn't find any words that wouldn't sound hollow, knowing what he knew about the machine's impending demise.

Arven seemed to sense his discomfort. 'I do not belong here,' he said, keeping his gaze fixed on the street beyond the grimy window. People were already milling around out there, going about their morning business.

'None of us belong here, Arven,' said Rory, quietly. 'But we have to stop the Squall. We have to find the Doctor and work out how to prevent them from sucking the planet dry, from killing any more people.'

Arven turned his scarred face from the window to look at Rory. The ribbons of torn flesh still hung across his left cheek like trailing fingers. 'I admire you, Rory Williams. I admire your resolve, your dedication. You remind me very much of Professor Gradius.'

Rory swallowed, unsure how to respond. 'Um, thanks.'

He turned, grateful for the interruption, at the sound of a boot scuffing the bare floorboards behind him. Amy stood watching them both with an amused expression on her face, her hands on her hips. 'OK, boys,' she said, full of gusto. 'It's a brand new day, and we're going to find the Doctor. Time to get moving!'

When the Squall found them again, they were down by the river.

Rory had suggested they head to the waterfront, at least in part because it was where he expected the day's events to transpire, unless things somehow played out very differently to how he imagined they would.

The Doctor knew that the AI would end up in the river at some point that day, too, so it seemed a reasonable assumption that he might come looking for them there. So Rory had led them to what he thought was roughly the same location at which they'd first arrived in London over a thousand years in the future. It was presently a nondescript spot on the embankment overlooking the Houses of Parliament. All had been quiet when they'd arrived, save for the pigeons that pecked incessantly at his boots and the squawking gulls that wheeled beneath a canopy of dirty grey, high above their heads.

Amy had clearly recognised where they were, but she'd remained steadfastly silent on the subject of Arven. To Rory this was a clear indicator that she suspected what was going to happen, but wasn't yet prepared to give voice to her thoughts.

Nevertheless, he felt somewhat guilty for hastening Arven on towards what would most likely prove to be the last few hours of his existence. Whether he was a machine or not, whether he actually experienced pain or anguish, he was still a person. Standing there on the embankment, looking out over the dark, glassy water, Rory had resolved to do whatever he could to save the AI, to alter the future, to prevent those things from coming to pass. Life wasn't predetermined. He knew that. Things *could* change. He'd seen the Doctor do it any number of times, plucking people out of their own timelines, saving people's lives, altering the course of events. Perhaps, then, there was hope for Arven? Perhaps.

Now, however, Rory was feeling a little less confident, as he backed up against the railing, clutching Amy's hand in his fist. Moments earlier a flock of Squall had descended in a grey flurry, swooping down on them from above. There were at least ten of them in the pack, and they didn't look as if they were about to take no for an answer.

Rory knew he should have been more prepared, should have been watching the skies, but the truth was that he was simply exhausted. Three days with hardly any food or sleep, remaining constantly on the run, had taken their toll. And now, it seemed, there was nowhere left for them to run. The Squall closed in on them, encircling them, hemming them in.

'You. Do. Not. Belong...' hissed the Squall in their broken, fragmented English. 'You. Taste... Different... The. Hive. Shall. Absorb. Your. Minds... The. Hive. Shall. Feast.'

Arven stepped forward, taking in each and every one of the aliens with a sweep of his head. 'No,' he said. 'This ends here.'

The Squall laughed, and it was one of the most hideous sounds that Rory had ever heard. 'The. Artificial. Man. Is. Of. No. Consequence... The. Hive. Shall. Feast.'

Was this it, then? Was this when Arven ended up in the river?

Rory was filled with a sudden sense of panic. He hadn't considered that he and Amy might end up the same way, dropped over the riverbank, their minds consumed by psychic parasites. Presently, it was looking like a distinct possibility.

Rory glanced at Amy, expecting one of her usual quips, but instead she simply grabbed hold of the back of his head, pulled him closer and planted a whopping great kiss on his lips.

'You too,' he said, turning back to the aliens.

There was nothing left to do. They were trapped, and the circle of Squall was closing.

Chapter
9

London, 17 October 1910

'See! Trouble. I told you. Always in trouble.'

The Doctor, grinning inanely, charged towards the gathering circle of Squall. 'Pond!' he bellowed at the top of his lungs. 'What do you think you're doing?'

'Doctor!' A woman's voice floated over the chittering of the alien beasts. 'Doctor! Over here!' She sounded triumphant and more than a little relieved to hear the Doctor's voice. She leapt up and down on the spot, waving her arms in the air above her head.

Angelchrist hurtled along behind the Doctor, keeping pace as best he could. It seemed odd to him that, after spending so much time running *away* from the alien creatures, the Doctor was now intent on haring *towards* them. Such was the way of this bizarre, impossible man; able, it seemed, to change his mind on a whim, to see at least three steps ahead of his opponents and take the necessary measures. Angelchrist decided he never wanted to challenge the man to a game of chess.

As they drew closer Angelchrist was able to make out three people at the heart of the trouble – a pretty young woman with bright red hair, a thin young man in a checked shirt and a tall, pale-skinned man wearing a black coat and cap. The first of these he assumed to be Amy, the Doctor's lady friend.

There were at least ten of the creatures encircling them, and they were backed up against the railing with nowhere to run. The Squall were closing in, clearly intent on devouring their minds.

The Doctor, of course, had very different thoughts on the matter. He skidded to a halt a couple of metres from the creatures, yanking his sonic screwdriver from his trouser pocket and jamming it into the receptacle at the base of his amplification device, which he clutched in his other hand. He poised his thumb over the button, ready to trigger the contraption.

'Oi! You lot! You've had your warning. Now get out of it. Go on. Get out of here.' The Doctor glared at the Squall, who turned as one to regard him, their glassy eyes shining in the morning sun. 'Leave my friends alone.'

'The. Hive. Knows. You. Doctor…' they replied. 'The. Squall. Have. Tasted. Your. Thoughts…. The. Hive. Hungers. For. Your. Mind.'

The Doctor shook his head. 'Ah, you see, that's where you've got it wrong. That's where you've got it very, very wrong. Because if you knew me, if the hive truly understood what I was about, it would know that I will never let it succeed, that I will do absolutely everything to prevent it from consuming this planet. It would know that I'm the Doctor, that I never give in, and that it should be very, very scared.' He paused, his expression stern, unforgiving. 'It would know that it should have left while it had the chance.'

The Squall cocked their heads to one side in a display of eerie symbiosis, regarding the Doctor as though weighing his words. 'The. Hive. Shall. Enjoy. Consuming. Your. Mind. Doctor... You. Are. A. Worthy. Enemy. Of. The. Squall...'

'Wrong answer!' said Amy, as the hungry pack of Squall turned away from her and launched themselves toward the Doctor, their talons glistening.

Calmly, the Doctor held his sonic device aloft and pressed the button. 'I warned you,' he said.

The results were instantaneous. The Squall dropped immediately to the ground like so many dead weights, screaming and writhing in agony. They clutched at their heads, some of them even using their own talons to burrow into their flesh as if trying to physically wrench the noise out of their heads.

Amy looked at the Doctor, a wide-eyed expression on her face.

The Doctor released the trigger. All around him, the grey-skinned creatures were sprawled on the ground, groaning and shaking their heads in confusion. 'Go. Now, before I press it again.'

The nearest Squall looked up at him and hissed, its fangs gleaming. Dark, red blood was trickling from its ears.

'Go!' he bellowed, and the creatures scattered, scrabbling over the paving stones and scampering away into the hazy morning. Seconds later, there was no sign that they'd ever been there at all.

The Doctor met Amy's gaze, a playful smile on his face. 'It won't keep them busy for long,' he said.

Amy's face split into the widest of grins and she ran at him, wrapping her arms around his shoulders and squeezing him tight. The Doctor, for his part, looked decidedly uncomfortable, and, with both hands full, simply stood there and allowed himself to be squeezed, a baffled expression on his face.

A moment later she released him, stepped back and folded her arms crossly over her chest, although Angelchrist could tell it was mock fury. 'Three days! Three days we've had to hang around waiting for you to show up. Do you know how desperately I need a shower?' She punched him gently on the arm. 'Three days!'

The Doctor glanced from Amy to the young man, and then back to Amy again. He gave her an apologetic look. 'I thought I left the two of you safely in the twenty-eighth century?' he said.

'Well, you left us in the twenty-eighth century,'

said the man. 'I'm not sure if safely is exactly the adjective I'd use to describe it.'

Angelchrist raised an eyebrow. The twenty-eighth century!

'The Squall,' said Amy. 'The Squall were there, too. We found Professor Gradius, but we were too late. They'd already killed her. We used her time ship to get away, to come back to 1910 to find you. Only, we overshot by a few days.'

'I'm sorry,' said the Doctor. 'I'm sorry I put you through that. Both of you.'

They stood in silence for a moment.

'Still,' said the Doctor, a little sheepishly, 'it must have been a *little* bit exciting, wasn't it? Travelling in an experimental time ship. Breaking new ground. You were probably some of the first humans in history to take part in an incredibly, *profoundly* dangerous time experiment. I mean, really, anything could have happened.' He prodded Amy inquisitively on the shoulder, then pinched her cheek between his finger and thumb as if checking she was actually real. Amy slapped his hand away and rubbed at her face. 'So? What was it like?'

Rory sighed. 'Fine. Good. Right up until the crash landing.'

'Ah. Yes. I saw that. Hmmm.' The Doctor tapped his index finger against his lips thoughtfully.

Feeling ever so slightly discomfited, as if he were intruding on a private conversation, Angelchrist gave a polite cough into his fist in an effort to remind the Doctor of his presence.

'Of course! How incredibly rude of me!' The Doctor spun around on the spot and beckoned him forward. 'Professor Angelchrist, meet Amy and Rory. Amy and Rory, say hello to Professor Angelchrist.' The Doctor took Angelchrist's hands, crossed them over the wrists and placed one of them in Amy's hand and the other in Rory's. He shook them all up and down and then stood back, looking pleased with himself.

They quickly released each other and stepped back, embarrassed expressions on their faces.

'Good. So we all know each another. Now we can get on with stopping the Squall,' said the Doctor. He turned as if to set off.

'Ah, wait a minute, Doctor,' said Angelchrist. 'I think you're forgetting someone.' The unusually tall man who was standing off to one side, quietly watching the retreating Squall, had piqued Angelchrist's curiosity.

'I am? Oh! Of course I am!'

Amy grinned, beckoning to the pale-skinned figure. He stepped forward so that the Doctor and Angelchrist could get a better look at him. 'This is Arven,' said Amy. 'He's a friend.'

Angelchrist regarded the unusual figure. At first his brain failed to register the ragged strips of flesh hanging loose from the man's face, or the dull, exposed metal of his cheekbone beneath. And then it hit him, and he almost staggered backward in surprise.

The man wasn't human.

'Ah, hello, Arven,' said Angelchrist, extending his hand.

The artificial man took it and shook it firmly. His hand felt rubbery and cold. 'Likewise, professor Angelchrist.'

The Doctor was grinning like a lunatic. 'Arven?' he said, with a knowing glance at Amy.

'My official designation is RVN-73,' replied Arven.

Angelchrist stepped out of the way to allow the Doctor through.

'Oh, look at *you*!' said the Doctor, giving Arven an appraising look. 'You're beautiful.' The Doctor walked in a circle around the AI, utterly transfixed. Then, coming around to face him again, he leaned in, studying Arven's face. 'Wonderful!' he said. 'Who built you?'

'My registered place of activation is the Villiers Artificial Life laboratory in Battersea, London.'

The Doctor nodded in appreciation. 'You were the pilot who brought my friends safely back to 1910?'

'Indeed,' said Arven, a glint in his eye.

'Well, thank you,' said the Doctor. 'But tell me, what happened to your arm?' he asked, peering nosily into the empty socket.

'Long story, involves a wall,' interrupted Rory. 'Let's just say my CV now states that I've performed an emergency amputation on a robot.'

'Oh, he's far more than a robot, Rory,' said the Doctor, patting Arven on the chest. 'Far more than that.' He turned, glancing over at Angelchrist. 'What time is it, professor?'

Angelchrist reached into his waistcoat pocket and extracted his timepiece. 'Just after ten,' he said.

The Doctor nodded. 'Then perhaps there's still time,' he said, more to himself than the others. He looked as if he were about to say something else, but Amy interrupted him with a question.

'Have you found the source? The hole where the Squall originated?' she said. 'You obviously haven't stopped them yet…'

'Yes. The rift was opened three days ago,' said the Doctor, distracted. 'The hive is growing in strength and… hold on a moment,' he looked momentarily taken back as her words finally registered, 'I've only been here a day!' The consternation was evident in his voice. 'A day! Not three, like some of us here.' He looked reprovingly at Rory, who raised his eyebrows in a 'what, me?' sort of way.

Amy frowned. 'Three days… but that's when we arrived, that's when… oh.' Angelchrist saw realisation dawn in her eyes. 'Oh. Oh no.'

'What is it?' said Rory, glancing nervously at the Doctor. 'What's wrong?'

'Three days, Rory! The rift opened three days ago. It was us…' Amy looked to the Doctor for confirmation, who gave her the slightest of nods. 'We were the ones who used the time ship to punch a hole through to 1910! We came in search of the Doctor. Arven even warned us. He said that until that point, the ship had only been used for short, local experiments. We're the ones responsible for allowing the Squall through to this time period in the first place.'

'Hang on a minute,' said Rory, raising a hand to ensure everyone was listening. 'I don't understand. How *can* it have been us? Surely that's some sort of paradox? We only came back in time to look for the Doctor because the Doctor came back looking for the monsters. The monsters were already here. That's right, isn't it?'

'Yes,' said the Doctor, 'but—'

'Hold on,' interrupted Rory. 'Let me get this straight. What you're describing is an impossibility. Logically, it can't have been us who opened the rift, because the rift already existed before we ever got into the time ship. Simple cause and effect. If it hadn't been for the AI in the river, you would never have gone back in time to find the Squall, and we would never have stayed behind in the twenty-eighth century.'

The Doctor shook his head. 'No, no, Rory. It doesn't work like that. History is like a…' the Doctor wove his fingers together and wiggled them around before Rory's face, searching for the right words, 'like a… a noodley soup of causality, a big bundle of threads. Pull a loose end and it begins to unravel. Events in the future impact on events in the past.' He glanced at Amy, and then turned his attention back to Rory again. Angelchrist stood watching him from the sidelines, a fascinated expression on his face.

'Humans experience the world in such a linear fashion. You live, you grow old, you die. But the universe is vaster and older and more complex than you could possibly imagine. History isn't linear, just because it seems that way. It's a living, changing thing. It shifts with the tides. History is more than the sum of what we experience, and it's not as fragile as you think. There are fixed points, yes,' he stopped for a moment to take a breath, 'things that *have* to happen, things that have occurred and will, always, occur. Those events can't change, can't be altered. Everything else... well, history flexes, Rory. Time bends. It tries to assert order on chaos.'

Rory frowned. 'So, just so I'm clear – the world isn't about to suddenly unravel because everything's stopped making sense?'

The Doctor looked deadly serious, as if Rory had asked the most momentous of questions and he'd honestly had to consider the answer. 'No. Reality isn't about to unravel. At least, I don't think so. For now. Assuming we can find a means of stopping the Squall, that is.' He ran a hand through his hair and screwed up his face in thought.

Rory didn't look at all placated by the answer he'd received.

Amy stepped forward, looping her arm through the Doctor's. 'So, what next, Doctor? I assume you have a plan?'

The Doctor smiled. 'You know me, Pond. I *always* have a plan.'

'That's what I'm worried about,' mumbled Rory.

'To the TARDIS!' proclaimed the Doctor, and set off, dragging Amy along beside him, his amplification device tucked safely beneath his left arm.

Shrugging, Angelchrist fell into step with the artificial man. Surely, he considered, things couldn't get any stranger than this.

Chapter
10

London, 17 October 1910

Angelchrist couldn't help but feel a slight sense of trepidation as the small troupe turned off the busy Cheyne Walk in the direction of the Doctor's ship. Just a few hours earlier the alleyway here had been the scene of a horrific attempt on the Doctor's life, and it was by sheer chance more than design that they'd been able to get away safely at all. The experience had not been a pleasant one, and Angelchrist was still smarting from his tumble across the cobbles.

Now, by returning so soon, it felt as if they were simply walking into a trap that had been knowingly laid on for them by the hive mind. Angelchrist hoped the move wasn't ill considered. He knew the Doctor needed to get back to his ship, but all the same, if it went wrong he'd be endangering the lives of several people. He hoped the Doctor really did have a plan.

He decided to forge ahead, and managed to catch the Doctor by the arm before he turned the corner into the mouth of the alleyway.

'Doctor, how do you know we're not simply walking into a trap?' he asked in hushed tones so the others wouldn't be startled.

'Oh, of course we're walking into a trap,' the Doctor replied, brightly. 'A big, fat, obvious trap. But the thing is, professor,' he leaned forward, conspiratorially tapping the side of his nose, 'we know it's a trap. And if we know it's a trap, it isn't really a trap at all.'

At this, he gave another of his beaming smiles, turned on his heel and disappeared around the corner in search of his ship.

Angelchrist couldn't quite follow the logic of the Doctor's assertion, but he was here now, and he couldn't in all good conscience allow the man to put himself in harm's way without offering his support. They'd been through so much together in just a few hours, and Angelchrist wasn't about to simply walk away just because the Doctor had managed to find his friends. London was still at risk. The *world* was still at risk, and Angelchrist knew his duty.

Facing his fear, he took a deep breath, fought against his instincts to flee, and followed the Doctor around the corner.

Sure enough, the alleyway was still crawling with the creatures. There were scores of them, covering almost every surface, like maggots writhing in a festering wound, like wasps in a vast and intricate hive, the TARDIS at the centre of it all, their cold, unwilling queen.

'Doctor...?' said Amy, moving over to stand beside him. There was hesitation in her tone. Nervousness. 'You said you had a plan?'

'Oh, don't worry, Amy,' said the Doctor. 'This sonic amplifier here is more than up to the task. Custom built for the purpose, in fact.'

The Doctor pulled the contraption out from under his arm, inserted the sonic screwdriver and held it aloft, pressing the button. 'There,' he said, satisfied.

Nothing happened.

'Hmmm... Now, I wasn't expecting *that*.'

'Doctor!' said Amy, now with a little more urgency. The Squall had begun to drop from their perches, scampering across the brickwork to get nearer to the Doctor, flowing towards them in an inexorable, chittering tide of grey.

Angelchrist stiffened, wishing he'd brought his revolver along after all, despite the Doctor's protestations. If he was going to die at the hands of these monsters, he at least wanted to go down fighting. He braced himself, waiting for the attack to come.

He heard a hissing sound from close behind him and turned to see a number of the Squall had come around behind their small group, hemming them in. Angelchrist edged closer to the Doctor, noticing that Rory and Arven were doing the same.

The Doctor pressed the button on his sonic

screwdriver again. Once again, nothing happened. 'Hmmm. That's interesting,' he said.

'What's interesting?' asked Amy, her tone growing in desperation. She was holding her head, groggy with the pain of the Squall's psychic assault.

'They're adapting faster than I anticipated,' he said. 'The hive is growing in intelligence. It won't be long before it's fully manifested. It's already figured out how to tune out the frequency of the sonic screwdriver.'

'Meaning?'

'Meaning the amplification device doesn't work.'

'So after all that, we're trapped?'

'Oh, I wouldn't put it quite like that, Amy. I'll think of something.'

'Well you'd better think quickly, Doctor,' said Rory, his back to them.

Angelchrist issued a cry of alarm as one of the creatures lurched for him, catching him by the jacket and causing him to stumble forward into the clutches of another. It wrapped its cold, bony fingers around his throat as he tried to fend it off, striking it repeatedly in the jaw with his fist and succeeding only in angering it further. He felt the thing probing at the edge of his consciousness and he cried out, mustering all of his strength in an attempt to defend himself.

'Doctor!' screamed Amy, distraught.

The Doctor glanced round to catch sight of

Arven, wrestling with one of the Squall, using his single remaining arm to keep it at bay by swinging it back and forth like a shield to block the progress of the others.

'Oh, Arven! You're a genius! Modulate the frequency! Why didn't I think of that?' The Doctor began to fumble with his contraption, pulling a bunch of wires loose and tying them together in a slightly different configuration.

'I don't understand, Doctor,' called the AI, its voice calm and steady, despite the ferocity of the battle in which it was engaged.

'Oh, just something you'll say to me when we first meet,' replied the Doctor. 'Hold on, professor!' he called to Angelchrist, 'Nearly there...'

'I can't hold them off much longer,' shouted Rory.

'Just a moment! Almost... almost... there!'

The Squall suddenly released its grip on Angelchrist's throat, shuddering and falling back against the wall of the alleyway. Angelchrist spluttered and fought for breath.

The Doctor brandished the device before him and the Squall parted in a great wave, falling back, screeching in frustration and pain. 'There,' he said. 'See how you like it when someone forces their way into your head. Not very nice, is it?'

'Come on,' he said to the others, stalking forward, cutting a swathe towards the TARDIS through the massed ranks of Squall.

He stopped before the doors, turning and handing

the crazed bundle of wires and components to Rory. 'Keep your finger on that button, Rory,' he said, and Rory nodded, nervously taking the contraption in both hands while trying to do as the Doctor asked.

The Doctor fished around in his pockets for a moment before producing a silver key, which he promptly dropped onto the cobbles and had to stoop to retrieve, an embarrassed twinkle in his eye. 'Always doing that,' he mumbled beneath his breath.

The Doctor turned the key in the latch and the TARDIS door swung open smoothly. 'Now,' he said magnanimously, 'come on inside, quickly.'

Angelchrist frowned. 'Doctor, how are we all going to fit in there?' Now that he was actually standing before the strange blue box – the Doctor's ship – Angelchrist felt utterly dismayed. With no Squall crawling over its surface he could see it clearly for the first time, and was shocked by the true dimensions of the thing. It was tiny, with room inside for no more than two or three people. 'There's no way we're all going to be able to squeeze inside.'

Amy, standing on the threshold, smiled back at him. 'Oh, I like this bit,' she said enigmatically.

'Trust me, professor,' said the Doctor, clapping him on the shoulder and urging him forward. 'You're going to enjoy this.'

Angelchrist, bemused, gave a brief nod of acknowledgement and followed Arven into the ship.

Inside, the room was enormous, entirely at odds with the dark, claustrophobic interior he'd expected. Instead, it was gleaming bright, all orange and red, like something out of a Jules Verne or H.G. Wells novel. The cavernous space seemed erratically designed, with various mezzanines connected by a network of walkways and staircases, disappearing off into what he presumed were other rooms within the ship. Strange, shining roundels were spaced at intervals around the walls, and at the heart of the room was a central dais – a large, raised platform – containing what Angelchrist could only assume were the vessel's controls. They reminded him of his laboratory, of the higgledy-piggledy contraption the Doctor had assembled there. They looked as if the Doctor had built them himself, patching them up out of whatever he had to hand. Perhaps, Angelchrist considered, that was exactly what had happened, and the control panel was nothing but a reflection of the Doctor's erratic, eccentric personality, of all the times and places he had visited.

He watched as the Doctor leapt up onto the platform, taking the stairs two at a time, and set to work banging at the controls, his fingers dancing over the myriad buttons and switches.

Angelchrist could barely fathom what he was seeing. There was a speaker from a gramophone; a typewriter; knobs, buttons, dials and levers; blinking glass screens that seemed to him like tiny windows, peering out onto other, unrecognisable worlds. There were looping cables; a chair; a hand crank; a bell; flashing lights. At the centre of it all was a tall glass column that extended up toward the distant ceiling, serving what purpose he could only imagine. And then there was the Doctor, presiding over it all like a mad man, a wide grin on his face as he threw himself into whatever task he had given his attention. It was impossible, and yet it was all maddeningly real.

Angelchrist reeled. Suddenly the strangeness of the last few hours, the sheer immensity of it all, came crashing in. He backed toward the door, feeling overwhelmed. He didn't know what to make of it. He turned, peering out of the door to see the alleyway beyond, the Squall still writhing there in their masses. Even that, somehow, seemed more real to him at that moment than the interior of the TARDIS. Even those monsters seemed easier to comprehend.

'Um... er...' he staggered toward the alleyway.

Amy caught him by the arm. 'I don't think you want to go back out there in a hurry, professor,' she said softly, pulling him in and slamming the door shut behind him.

'But...?'

'I know, it's a lot to take in,' she said.

'This is your ship, Doctor? Your vessel?'

'Yes! Marvellous, isn't it?' called the Doctor, still intent on hammering away at the vessel's controls.

'It's miraculous! It's... it's...'

'Big?' offered Rory.

Angelchrist laughed out loud, twisting around

on the spot, trying to take it all in. 'Yes!' he said. 'Yes, it's big!'

He felt breathless. His heart was hammering in his chest so that he thought it might burst. 'How…?' he said, trailing off, unable to find the words.

'Dimensionally transcendental,' called the Doctor from over by the console. He was hopping about now, still twiddling dials and examining readouts.

'Or in other words, bigger on the inside,' said Rory, grinning.

'Bigger on the inside,' Angelchrist repeated. 'Quite so.'

'Professor Gradius would have marvelled,' said Arven, circling the room, staring up at the gleaming central column. 'This was always her dream. A vessel such as this.' He sounded full of awe.

'What wonders,' said Angelchrist, 'what remarkable things you must have seen…'

'Oh, you get used to it,' said Amy, nonchalantly, as she skipped up the steps toward the Doctor. 'And sometimes the plumbing leaves something to be desired.'

The Doctor glanced up, shooting her an affronted look. 'Now, let's see about this dimensional rift, shall we?' He grasped hold of the edges of a monitor screen and pulled it closer to him on concertinaed hinges, examining its contents intently. 'Oh,' he said, after a moment. 'Oh, that's not good. That's not good at all.'

'What is it?' said Amy.

'It's too big,' he replied, his voice low and serious.

'The rift is too big. It's a whopping great hole in the fabric of the universe. So big you could get a double decker bus through it.' He seemed to shudder at the very thought of this. 'Actually, I've done that before. Not a pleasant experience.'

'Too big for what?' asked Angelchrist.

'I was planning to use the TARDIS,' said the Doctor. 'Fly it through the rift, cause it to collapse in on itself. But the hole is too wide. The stress would cause the TARDIS to implode.'

'Um…' said Rory, and everyone turned to regard him. 'Forgive me for stating the obvious, but that's a bad idea, isn't it?'

'I'm guessing we might need a new plan?' said Amy.

'What *would* happen,' said Angelchrist, watching the Doctor intently. 'If the TARDIS were to implode.'

'Oh, you know. End of the universe, cracks through time. Same old story. Wouldn't want to go through *that* again.'

The Doctor stood back from the console, drumming his fingers against his temples. He paced back and forth while the others looked on in silence.

'So?' said Amy, after a moment, 'what about Plan B?'

'Plan B?' said the Doctor. 'Plan B? Yes. Good point. There's always a Plan B.'

'And…?' she coaxed.

'And… I'm working on it,' he said, with a sigh.

He crossed to one of the railings, and then returned to the console again, his forehead wrinkled in thought.

'DOCTOR.' The voice came suddenly, booming loudly throughout the TARDIS and causing all but Arven and the Doctor to cringe, covering their ears in surprise at the sudden aural assault. 'DOCTOR,' it sounded again, and this time it was immediately clear to whom the sinister, hissing voice belonged.

'Doctor! That's the Squall. How are they doing that?' said Amy, urgently. 'Are they in the TARDIS?'

'Oh, you're clever,' said the Doctor, addressing the voice. 'You're very, very clever.' Angelchrist could hear the admiration in his voice.

'Doctor?' said Rory.

'It's using the TARDIS's telepathic circuits, manipulating the ship's psychic matrix. The hive mind is talking to us through the TARDIS,' he said.

'WE SEE, DOCTOR, THAT WE WERE RIGHT TO CONSIDER YOU A WORTHY OPPONENT,' the voice boomed.

The Doctor laid a hand on the console. 'I'm sorry old girl,' he whispered. 'Might be nice if you could keep it down a bit,' he called to the hive mind.

'WE RELISH THE OPPORTUNITY TO ABSORB YOUR MIND, DOCTOR. THE TIME IS APPROACHING. YOUR TARDIS WILL BE A GREAT ASSET TO THE HIVE. WE SHALL POPULATE THE UNIVERSE, EXTENDING OURSELVES INTO EVERY CONCEIVABLE TIME

AND PLACE IN THIS PHYSICAL REALM.'

'So *that's* why you're so anxious to consume my mind,' said the Doctor. 'Oh, you disappoint me. You really do. I'd have thought you'd have come up with something a bit more original than that. Well, I can assure you, I won't allow it. Whatever happens, I won't let you have the TARDIS.'

The Squall laughed, and the sound of it made Angelchrist's stomach churn. 'YOU HAVE NO CHOICE. THIS CITY WILL FALL WITHIN A FEW HOURS. THE HIVE IS MANIFESTING. THIS UNIVERSE WILL BE OURS.'

'Doctor, what are we going to do?' said Amy. There was desperation in her tone. For the first time since meeting her, Angelchrist got the sense that, despite the bravado, despite the gallant front, she was really just as fragile and scared as the rest of them. With the exception, perhaps, of the unflappable Doctor himself.

The Doctor met her gaze across the console. 'We're going to stop them,' he said, decisively. 'That's what we're going to do. With the TARDIS, the Squall would be unstoppable. They would spread like a plague, right across the universe, obliterating not only every world, but every known point in time, too. Species would cease to exist in the blink of an eye. Only the hive would exist, all pervading, all knowing.' The Doctor turned to Angelchrist. 'Professor, we need to get back to your lab.'

'Very well, Doctor,' he replied, pleased to be able to offer at least some assistance.

'But the creatures,' said Arven. 'They're swarming all over the ship. Even with your amplification device, I'm doubtful we'll be able to deter them all.'

The Doctor grinned. 'Then we'll take the shortcut,' he said, reaching over to the console. He punched a few buttons and yanked on a lever, and the ship bucked suddenly beneath their feet. 'Hold on!' he called.

There was a grating, wheezing roar from within the belly of the TARDIS, and Angelchrist was pitched forward, clutching for a nearby railing as the floor seemed to lurch, first one way and then another. The glass column at the centre of the console rose and fell in keeping with the steady sighing of the ship. Angelchrist held on for all he was worth.

Moments later there was a resounding *clang*, and everything was still.

Chapter

11

London, 17 October 1910

'Right!' said the Doctor, giving a brisk clap of his hands. 'We've arrived.'

Amy, peeling herself away from where she'd been gripping the console, jumped down from the central dais and ran over to where Rory was standing beside Arven.

Angelchrist looked on in confusion. 'What? Have we moved? Are you telling me this vessel has just flown us halfway across London, all in a matter of a few seconds?'

'Absolutely!' said the Doctor, brightly. 'We're in your laboratory, professor. I'm afraid I'm going to need to raid your workshop again.'

'Oh... ah... be my guest,' said Angelchrist, feeling more than a little baffled by the whole situation. *In his laboratory?* Surely not? How could a vehicle arrive suddenly *indoors*?

He watched as Amy strode purposefully toward the door, turned the latch and disappeared outside. 'Oh, nice pad, professor,' she said, her voice trailing behind her through the open door. She popped her head back around the doorframe. 'You coming?' she said to Rory.

Tentatively, Angelchrist released his grip on the railing, which he realised he'd been gripping so hard that his knuckles had gone white. He flexed his fingers, trying to get the feeling back. He'd never been a nervous man, taking everything he encountered in his stride. He'd fought monsters on behalf of the British government, both men and beasts, and he'd travelled halfway around the globe, immersing himself in wildly different cultures. But this... travelling in a vessel such as this... Well, he didn't know what to make of it. He felt speechless, as if his world had just been turned upside down.

'Go on, professor. It's all right, really,' said the Doctor, coming over to stand beside him and putting a reassuring hand on his shoulder.

Angelchrist allowed himself to be led to the door. He peered out nervously through the opening.

Sure enough, he could see his laboratory on the other side. He smiled at the familiar sight of his armchair beside the bookcase; the coffee table, still strewn with the tools and equipment abandoned there by the Doctor earlier that morning; the Egyptian sarcophagus standing proud against the far wall; even his prized clockwork owl, hopping from foot to foot on its wooden perch, clacking and chirping.

He stepped out over the threshold, relieved to feel his feet encounter the plush, red carpet. He filled his nostrils with the musty scent. Yes, he was in his laboratory. It was unmistakable. He glanced back at the Doctor stepping out of the TARDIS behind him. 'It's a miracle,' he said, 'an out and out miracle! This... this box of tricks – it's the work of a magician!'

The Doctor grinned, leaning in the doorway. 'A magician? I think I could take to that,' he said.

'Oh, leave him alone, professor. He's got a big enough head as it is,' said Amy playfully.

'Oi! Watch it, Pond,' said the Doctor, stepping out to allow Arven to join the others. He turned and patted the wooden frame of the police box. 'I don't know what I'd do without her,' he added. 'And I suppose it is magic, of a sort.'

Angelchrist smiled. 'Thank you, Doctor,' he said.

He crossed the room to where Amy and Rory were milling about, examining the decades' worth of paraphernalia.

'It's the ultimate boy's room,' said Rory, clearly entranced by the spoils of so many adventures. He was running his hands over a clay tablet that had been impressed with a letter to the gods, written in ancient cuneiform. Amy was watching him with adoring eyes.

Arven, on the other hand, was silently taking it

all in. He seemed the most ill at ease of them all, this mechanical man, as if he knew he didn't belong in this world, in this age of steam and industry. He was an oddity here, an anachronism, unable to understand his surroundings, unable to blend in like the others.

There was something else, too. Angelchrist was sure of it. The automaton appeared to be afflicted by a great sense of loss. Whether this was a symptom of being so dramatically displaced in time – he'd overheard the Doctor claim that Arven was a relic from the twenty-eighth century – or whether there was something deeper, something more personal behind it, Angelchrist did not know. He didn't suppose there was a great deal he could do to help.

Angelchrist glanced back at the TARDIS. From here, the wooden box looked as if it might always have been a fixture in his laboratory, standing there between the remnants of a Grecian marble and the wooden model of the Neanderthal man. Just another oddity in his collection.

That was the difference between the Doctor and Arven, he considered. Not the fact that one was formed from flesh and blood and the other from steel and rubber, but the fact that the Doctor just seemed to *fit*. For him it seemed effortless – the manner in which he'd ingratiated himself in Angelchrist's life, the way in which he talked to people – even the way he'd dealt with the Squall. He, too, was from another time and place, but seemed eminently adaptable, able to compensate as he went, comfortable with his incongruities. It was admirable, and spoke to Angelchrist of great experience. He wondered how old the Doctor really was.

Right now, the Doctor was busying himself gathering armfuls of components from around the lab. He bustled about like this for a few moments, making interested noises as he added to his pile of bits. Then, sighing happily like a child in a sweet shop, he plumped himself down in an armchair and scattered bits of metal and reels of copper wire all over the coffee table. Next, he produced the amplification device he'd made earlier, along with Angelchrist's best top hat.

'Rory,' he said, without looking up from the heaped mess, through which he'd already begun to rifle with apparent purpose, 'I'm going to need a few bits from the TARDIS, too.'

'Anyone for tea?' asked Angelchrist, suddenly remembering his manners. There were more visitors in his house than he'd seen in years, and the momentary disorientation of having travelled in the Doctor's extraordinary vessel had thrown him.

'Excellent idea,' said the Doctor, 'that's exactly what's called for.'

'And food,' said Amy, hopefully. 'If you have any food? It's been three days since our last proper meal.'

'Of course,' said Angelchrist, nodding. 'I'll see what I can rustle up. Mr Arven?' he asked, unsure of the etiquette. 'Is there anything you require?'

'No, thank you, professor. There is nothing I

require at this time,' came the monotone reply.

Angelchrist imagined there was rather a lot the artificial man required, but nothing that he or anyone else in the room could offer. 'Very well. Please, make yourselves at home,' he said, redundantly. 'I'll return in a few moments.'

As he made his way to the kitchen, Angelchrist considered the events of the last day. He couldn't quite believe that he was worrying about domestic duties at a time like this, only minutes after being attacked in an alleyway down by the river and with vast hordes of Squall infesting London. But, just as the Doctor had said, it seemed to be exactly what was called for. He would do his bit. He would make himself useful, whatever it was that needed doing.

When Angelchrist returned ten minutes later bearing a plate of hastily prepared sandwiches and a full pot of tea, he found the Doctor and Arven sitting by the coffee table, deep in discussion. Amy and Rory were still poking around amongst the detritus of his secret service career, pawing through the heaps of miscellaneous junk looking for treasure. It amused him to see young people so fascinated by his collection. To many of their age it would appear as nothing but so much rubbish, the accumulation of a lifetime spent refusing to throw anything away.

To him, of course, it was priceless, regardless of its monetary value. All of it. To him, each and every object was a memory, a part of his life, a fragment of what he'd once been and what he'd never be again.

The thought saddened him, a little. Was that really what his life had come to? A heap of old junk in a lonely house in Grosvenor Square? He'd never married, always too busy to give romance more than a cursory thought. Had he thrown his life away? Had he wasted his best years chasing around after the enemies of Great Britain, only to lose everything now, to the Squall?

Perhaps it wasn't true. Perhaps he was just being maudlin. The Doctor had shown him he still had some fire left in his belly and, by jove, the Squall would bear the brunt of it, even if it finished him off.

He had faith in the Doctor, too, he realised. He couldn't explain why, but he trusted the man implicitly. There was something about him, some facet of his exuberant, frustrating personality that inspired Angelchrist to keep on fighting. And fight he would, right up until the bitter end.

For now, though, he had a job to do.

Angelchrist took the tray over to Amy and Rory and they turned their attention gratefully to the food, making quick work of the sandwiches. He then poured the tea and went over to join the Doctor and Arven, whose conversation seemed to have stuttered to a halt. The Doctor was still busy fiddling with the pile of odds and ends on the table, wiring two components together with a bizarre tool that looked more like a fork with three glowing nibs than anything one might use to construct something.

'Doctor? You were talking earlier as if we'd met before,' said Arven, 'but I have no recollection of these events. Could it be that you're mistaken?'

The Doctor, his eyes fixed on whatever delicate transaction was taking place between the two wires he held in his fingers, gave a resigned sigh, as if he'd been waiting for the AI to ask this very question. 'We have met before, Arven. In the future. In your time. You helped,' he said.

'I do not understand,' continued the artificial man.

'It's complicated, Arven. The TARDIS can travel in time as well as space, just like Professor Gradius's ship. Well, much more successfully than Professor Gradius's ship, really, but that's beside the point,' he said, popping the pencil-thing between his teeth while he manhandled the object on his lap. 'Events that will occur in your future have already occurred in my past,' he said, shaping the words slowly around the tool in his mouth.

Angelchrist raised an eyebrow at this, but decided not to chip in.

'So I make it home?' said Arven, and Angelchrist marvelled that a machine could express so much emotion with a simple expression, despite its damaged face. It was far more than sheer mimicry, of that he was sure.

The Doctor paused in his ministrations and looked up. 'You take the long way home, Arven,' he said, cryptically, and the look in his eye was enough to tell the AI that the matter was closed. The

Doctor returned his attention to the device in his lap, manipulating a coil of copper wire into place, affixing it to the framework of what had once been his amplification device.

'What are you doing, Doctor?' asked Angelchrist, as much to break the awkward silence as anything else.

'Oh, just making a few improvements,' said the Doctor. 'A modification here or there.' To Angelchrist, the construction looked more bizarre and more unprofessional than ever.

He was about to ask the Doctor what the device was intended to do, when a voice boomed suddenly from the TARDIS, ringing out through the open doors and causing Angelchrist to wince in pain. 'DOCTOR. THE TIME APPROACHES. SOON YOU SHALL BE OURS.'

'Hard work, being popular,' said the Doctor, with a defiant wink at Angelchrist. 'I'm sorry, professor. They're here. We've brought them to your home.'

'It's not your fault, Doctor. There's nothing else you could have done.' He turned at the sound of talons tapping menacingly at the window, the *scritch-scratch* of the creatures on the roof, at the walls, at the doors. 'We make a stand. Right here,' he said.

'All you need to do is hold them off,' said the Doctor. 'Just keep them at bay for a few more minutes.'

Arven stood and crossed to the window. 'There are hundreds of them,' he said, his voice level.

'They're swarming all over the house.'

From somewhere upstairs came the crash of broken glass.

'Defend yourselves!' called Angelchrist, rising to his feet and rushing over to a glass-fronted display cabinet on the wall. He pulled open the doors and grasped hold of a mediaeval mace, hefting it in his hands, comforted by its weight, the feel of its shaft.

'They're getting more sophisticated,' said the Doctor. 'As the hive grows in strength, the drones are becoming more and more intelligent. Be careful.'

The laboratory door shuddered violently in the frame, followed by the sinister *scritch, scritch* of one of the creatures trying to get in. Amy stumbled backwards, away from the door. She grabbed hold of a bronze idol of the Buddha that Angelchrist had acquired twenty years earlier during one of his trips to the East. She raised it above her head, ready to use it if the creature managed to break through.

Seconds later the window shattered and Arven called out as he struck at the Squall attempting to force its way through the ragged hole. He wrapped his remaining hand around its face and pushed it back, sending it sprawling to the street outside. But seconds later there were two more of the creatures, and Angelchrist rushed to his aid, swinging the mace with all of his strength. It connected with a flashing talon, and Angelchrist felt the satisfying crunch of shattered bone.

'Hurry up, Doctor! Whatever you're doing,' he called, as he heard Amy scream over to his left.

He turned to see her slamming the Buddha down across the shoulders of a Squall who had finally managed to splinter the panelled door and force its way through. It crumpled to the floor and didn't move.

Rory was standing by her side, the Neanderthal's wooden club clutched tightly in his hands. He swung it with a terrified 'Arrgghhhh' as another of the creatures jammed its head through the fragmented door.

'YOUR ATTEMPTS TO DEFEND YOURSELF ARE FUTILE,' said the voice from the TARDIS. 'THE HIVE SEES ALL. THE HIVE KNOWS ALL. WE ARE LEGION.'

'Ignore it!' called the Doctor. 'Don't let it get to you.'

'That's proving rather difficult,' said Rory through gritted teeth, as he jammed his elbow into the face of a Squall while Amy threw priceless fragments of Roman mosaic at another.

'Nearly there!' called the Doctor. 'Almost...'

'I can't hold them off for much longer!' called Arven from the window.

'There! Finished!' said the Doctor. Angelchrist turned to see the Doctor stood, his arms held wide, the top hat perched atop his mop of unruly hair. 'What do you think?' he said.

'What have I told you about hats!' said Amy, grunting as, together, she and Rory manoeuvred the ancient wooden sarcophagus across the doorway to form a barricade. Angelchrist sighed at the loss as one of the creature's talons burst through what was left of the door, raking great furrows in the decorated outer coffin.

'It's a top hat!' said the Doctor. 'Top hats are cool. Particularly *this* top hat,' he added, lifting it off by the rim to reveal a bundle of intricate wires and components nestling inside.

'What is it?' cried Rory, with a tone somewhere between exasperation and desperation.

'This?' said the Doctor. 'This is Plan B.'

Chapter
12

London, 17 October 1910

'Well don't just stand there! Use it!' shouted Amy, rolling her eyes at the Doctor as he popped the hat back onto his head and retrieved his sonic screwdriver from amongst the pile of scraps on the table.

'Ah, well. Yes. That's the problem. You see, it's not quite as simple as all that.'

'What do you mean?' shouted Angelchrist over the noise of the hissing creatures at the window, swinging the mace to send another of them spinning back out into the street. 'You said you were just making a few improvements. Can't you use it to repel the Squall?'

The Doctor looked sheepish. 'Well, those improvements I mentioned... It's more that, now, it'll have quite the opposite effect.'

'You mean that thing will actually *attract* the

creatures?' said Amy, the disbelief evident in her voice. '*Doctor*…'

'Yes. You see, the Squall want the TARDIS. And the only person on this planet who knows how to pilot the TARDIS is me. Ergo…'

'They want you,' said Amy. 'But we already knew that.'

'Oh, Amy, it's much better than that. To the hive, my mind is the tastiest morsel in the universe right now. So tasty, in fact, that every single one of those drones out there is trying to get at it. They've had a taste of it, you see, back in the alleyway yesterday, and they've seen what's on offer. None of your typical human minds, thank you very much.' The Doctor paused for a moment. 'As pleasant as those human minds might be,' he added quickly. 'No, the hive has seen inside the mind of a Time Lord, and it wants to get at the secrets locked within.'

'This is all fascinating stuff, Doctor, but what does it actually *mean*?' said Rory, still working to barricade the door by piling up more and more of Angelchrist's archaeological treasures.

'The hat will boost my mind's psychic signal. Amplify it to epic proportions. It'll be like a beacon to all of the Squall in the city. They won't be able to resist. They'll come flocking. When I turn this little beauty on… Well, if you think there's a lot of them here now, just you wait.'

'And that helps us *how*?' said Amy, perplexed.

'It means I can lead them to wherever I want them to be,' said the Doctor, grinning. 'It means I can get them all back to the rift. Every one of them. The signal from the hat will call to them, far and wide.'

'Like the pied piper of Hamlyn,' said Angelchrist, 'leading the rats to their doom.' He had to admit, he was impressed with the Doctor's audacity.

'Well,' said the Doctor, a little disapprovingly, 'more like sending them back to where they belong.'

'But how are you going to do that?' asked Amy. 'You said it was too dangerous to close the rift with the TARDIS.'

'It is,' said the Doctor. 'But there's another time ship in 1910. A damaged, experimental time ship that might just have enough of a kick left in it to seal the rift.'

Amy frowned. 'So you're going to create an implosion? You're going to lead all of the Squall right the way across London to the rift, and basically cause the time ship to blow up, sending them all back to their own dimension on the other side of time? Just, so, you know, I'm getting this right.'

'Boom!' said the Doctor, grinning insanely and making an explosive gesture with his fingers.

'I love Plan B!' said Amy, laughing out loud. 'Yay for Plan B!'

'So, what now?' said Rory. 'Back in the TARDIS, short hop across town?'

The Doctor shook his head.

'No?' said Rory. 'No. Of course not. Things are never that simple.'

'The TARDIS is compromised,' said the Doctor

sadly. 'The hive is almost fully manifested. I can't risk taking her anywhere now. There are so many Squall in the vicinity that the hive mind might be able to assert an influence, altering her course, or worse.' He walked over to his ship and pulled the doors to. 'Besides, we can't risk her being inadvertently sucked into the temporal implosion. We have to keep her clear of the dimensional rift.'

The Doctor glanced at Angelchrist, and then turned back to face the TARDIS once more. 'Then again...' he said, trailing off in thought. He pushed open the doors and slipped inside. Angelchrist could hear his footfalls echoing as he ran to the central console, followed by the sounds of frenetic button pushing and the cranking of levers. Then, a few seconds later, he emerged with a smile on his face, pulling the doors shut behind him with a flourish. 'Right, where were we?' he said, a little out of breath.

'Professor, help me with this,' said Arven, and Angelchrist looked round to see the AI dragging a tall mahogany dresser across the window. 'We can make a temporary barricade. It won't last long but it might give us some time.' He appeared to be ignoring the talons that were flashing through the shattered window, rending great clumps of flesh out of his back.

Angelchrist and Rory fell in, helping to slide the heavy piece of furniture into place. They pushed it up against the window with a final, momentous heave, blotting out the light and casting everything in inky shadows.

'If we can't use the TARDIS, Doctor, how *are* we going to get to the time ship?' said Amy.

The Doctor rubbed a hand over his chin. 'Oh, plenty of options yet,' he said.

'Forgive me, Doctor,' said Angelchrist, 'but I can't see how any of us are getting out of this house. At least not alive. There're simply too many of the ruddy things.'

'Good point, professor,' said the Doctor, wagging his finger. 'Very good point. The odds are certainly stacked against us.' He paused, as if considering. 'But that's never stopped me before. And anyway, there's one thing we have going for us that the Squall don't. One *little* thing that could make all the difference.'

'What?' asked Angelchrist.

'Your car,' said the Doctor, beaming. 'Wonderful machine. True vintage. Perfect for a jaunt across town.'

The dresser by the window shifted suddenly with an enormous bang, as the Squall began to hurl themselves bodily at the barricade. 'It won't hold for very long,' reiterated Arven. 'They'll be through any minute.'

'Tell me if I'm being stupid, Doctor, but to use the car, don't we first have to get to it?' said Rory.

'Yes,' replied the Doctor.

'And isn't it parked on the other side of the street?'

'Yes,' the Doctor repeated. 'Quiet now. Thinking.'

He paced back and forth around the room, looking faintly ridiculous in his tweed jacket, bow tie and top hat.

'I'll do it,' announced Arven with sudden urgency, and the Doctor stopped pacing and looked up, a concerned expression on his face. 'I'll create a distraction,' Arven continued. 'If I make a run for it, they might give chase. At least for a moment. It could buy you enough time to get to the car.'

The Doctor looked thoughtful. 'No, Arven. I can't allow you to do that. They'd tear you apart.'

Arven met the Doctor's gaze. 'The long way home, Doctor,' he said. 'I don't belong here. At least allow me to help with this.'

'No,' said Rory, stepping forward as if to block Arven's path to the door. 'Doctor?'

The Doctor sighed.

'*Doctor!*' said Amy. 'He can't!'

'What choice do we have?' said the Doctor. 'The professor's right. Unless we can get to that car, there's no way out of this house. There are too many lives at stake.' He reached inside his jacket pocket and extracted his sonic screwdriver. He approached Arven, running the glowing tip of the sonic over the AI's chest plate.

'What are you doing?' said the AI.

'Oh, just a couple of minor adjustments. Nothing to worry about. They'll make it easier for the TARDIS to home in on you later.'

'Your past, my future,' said Arven, with a crooked grin. Angelchrist thought it was the first time he'd seen the artificial man smile.

'Something like that,' replied the Doctor, gravely. He reached up and patted the AI on the shoulder.

Angelchrist studied the pale figure of the AI as he turned to Rory and Amy. 'Thank you,' he said. 'For everything.'

Rory stepped forward and took the machine's hand in his own. 'Until later.'

Amy leapt up and wrapped her arms around Arven's neck, clutching him to her. 'See you in a thousand years,' she said.

Finally, the AI turned to Angelchrist. 'It's been a pleasure, professor.'

'Likewise, Arven,' he replied.

With some dignity, Arven approached the door and began pulling aside the barricade, attempting to lift the sarcophagus with one arm. Angelchrist looked on, stirred by the machine's bravery as Rory went to Arven's aid, helping him to lift the coffin away. At that point, the AI seemed more human to Angelchrist than any number of scoundrels he'd had to contend with over the years. More human, even, than the enigmatic Doctor.

The Squall crowding the doorway took advantage of the sudden break in the defences and began to force their way in, their claws scrabbling to find purchase on Arven's artificial flesh. He barely seemed to notice as he forced his way into their midst, thrashing out at them, slapping them away as he fought his way towards the door.

A moment later he was gone, lost amidst a forest

of thrashing grey limbs.

As they'd hoped and anticipated, the Squall in the hallway rushed after him, creating a momentary lull in their siege.

'Now!' said the Doctor. 'Make it count.'

Together, the four of them charged out through the ruins of the laboratory door, Rory still clutching the Neanderthal's club, Angelchrist still clinging on to his mace.

'Through here,' called Angelchrist, leading them on toward the kitchen. 'There's another way out.' He could hear the Squall chittering and hissing frantically as they set upon the AI in the street outside. He cringed at the thought of what they would do to him. He would do as the Doctor suggested. He would make Arven's sacrifice count.

Above them, he could hear the Squall still banging around on the upper floor, piling in through the shattered windows, trying to cut off their escape routes, trying to hem them in. Well, his old house had a few tricks up its sleeve that the alien interlopers might not be expecting.

Angelchrist skidded to a halt before a white wooden door. 'Down there!' he said, flinging it open and indicating the stone stairwell.

'The cellar?' said Rory, confused. 'I thought we were trying to get out of here?'

Angelchrist nodded, panting for breath. 'Yes. There's an access point at the side of the house. It leads right down to the cellar. We can shimmy our way up and out.'

'Good!' said the Doctor, thundering down the steps. 'Excellent!' The others followed suit, and Angelchrist brought up the rear, pulling the door shut behind him.

It was dark and dank down there and smelled of damp earth and mould. The Doctor pulled his sonic screwdriver from his pocket and held it aloft, shining it like a torch, lighting their way.

Angelchrist pushed his way to the front, leading them through a maze of wooden crates and boxes; more accumulated junk from his old life. He'd hardly stepped down there for years, and could barely remember the contents of most of the neatly stacked parcels. He supposed in a very real sense he'd moved on from that life of adventure, growing old and careworn, despite continuing to poke his nose in the business of the police, despite surrounding himself with the relics upstairs in the lab.

He was now himself nothing but a relic, an old soldier, a half-remembered footnote in the stories of the great men. The Doctor had changed all of that, though. The Doctor had waltzed into his life like a bumbling, ungainly teenager, sweeping him up into his insane adventure, instilling him with renewed vigour and life. The Doctor had reminded Angelchrist what it was to be alive. He was damned if he was going to let a few wretched parasites spoil that for him now.

'Over here,' said Angelchrist, pointing up to a small access hatch in the ceiling.

'How are we going to get up there?' asked Amy.

'Pull some of these boxes a bit closer,' said Rory, grabbing a handful of crates and stacking them quickly against the wall. Together, the four of them began piling more and more of the boxes on top of each other, forming a makeshift platform from which they could reach the trapdoor above.

The Doctor was first to leap up onto it, craning his neck so that his ear was close to the wooden hatch. 'Sounds like they're still busy,' he said. He gripped the sonic screwdriver between his teeth and reached up with both hands, giving the trapdoor a sharp shove. It creaked and gave way, sprinkling him with a shower of dust and grit.

'Pah!' the Doctor spluttered, rubbing his face in the crook of his elbow and pulling a dismayed face. He tapped the fragments from the brim of his top hat – his *best* top hat, Angelchrist reminded himself – and slid the trapdoor slowly to one side. Daylight slanted in through the small opening.

Without further ado, the Doctor jumped up, grasped the sides of the hole and pulled himself through, snaking his hips through the slight opening. Angelchrist watched from below, waiting anxiously to see what would happen. He could hear the Squall from outside, still hissing and wrenching away bits of his beloved home.

There was no sign of the Doctor. Angelchrist saw Amy and Rory exchange a worried glance. Then the Doctor's face appeared in the opening, his expression reminiscent of an excited schoolboy, and the sense of relief in the cellar was almost palpable.

'Coast's clear,' he said. 'Well, sort of.' He beckoned to Amy. 'Come on, Pond.'

Amy scrambled up onto the pile of boxes and extended her arms toward the Doctor. He reached down and clasped her around the forearms, heaving her up with a slight groan of exertion.

'Now you, Rory,' he said a moment later, reappearing at the hole.

Finally, with one last, mournful glance back at his home, Angelchrist climbed onto the shaky stack of boxes and allowed the Doctor and Rory to heave him up into the dazzling sunshine outside.

The sight out there was horrific, worse than he could have ever imagined. His house was crawling with the creatures. They covered every conceivable part of its surface, relentlessly dismantling it brick by brick, tile by tile. There were *thousands* of them. He could see them forcing their way in through the windows, prising away the wooden frames and sending them tumbling to the ground below. They had smashed a hole in the roof and a torrent of them was pouring in through the gaping wound, flowing through into his home, like liquid being poured into a glass.

Outside, in the street, was Arven, now reduced to little more than a gleaming metal skeleton, still thrashing about, still fending them off as more and more of the creatures leapt upon him, attempting to pull his remaining arm from its socket.

'Quickly,' said the Doctor. He pointed across the street to where Angelchrist's vehicle was parked.

Haring over to it, he vaulted up and over the door and into the driver's seat.

For a moment Rory looked as if he was about to start forward, to run to Arven's aid, but Amy grabbed his arm and dragged him towards the waiting vehicle. They clambered up into the rear seats, and Angelchrist, distraught and still clutching his mace, ran around the front and hurriedly gave the crank handle a sharp twist.

The engine sputtered, but didn't start.

'Oh, you've got to be kidding!' said Amy.

One of the nearby Squall, squatting on a railing, cocked its head and turned slowly to look at them. Its beady red eyes flashed in recognition, and it leapt from its perch, spreading its membranous wings and gliding toward them.

'Don't look now,' said Angelchrist, 'but it knows we're here.'

As one, the heads of all the Squall on the side of the building turned to regard them.

'Go!' Amy yelled.

The Squall that had been squatting on the railing crashed down onto the bonnet of the car, crumpling one of the headlights, its talons puncturing the thin metal hood. Angelchrist stood, swinging his mace at the monster as it tried to scramble up and over the windscreen to get at the Doctor. It ducked neatly out of the way of his blow, cracking the windscreen with its claws.

'Come on, professor!' called the Doctor.

Desperately, Angelchrist cranked the handle

again. This time the engine took, roaring to life with a mechanical rattle.

'There's more of them coming!' called Rory from the back seat.

The Doctor slammed his foot on the accelerator and the car shot forward, sending the Squall tumbling over the side, bouncing off the runner board. Angelchrist dived out of the way, and Rory leaned over, catching him by the arms as he fell and hauling him up into the passenger seat as they roared off down the street.

The creatures were harrying them from all sides now, and the Doctor weaved the car around erratically on the road. Whether he was trying to avoid them or simply throw them off, Angelchrist couldn't be sure. Either way, it didn't appear to be working.

He glanced back at his house as they barrelled along the road, to see Arven, finally subdued, being carried away into the sky by two bickering Squall. They were tearing indiscriminately at his remaining limbs in an attempt to rend him apart, allowing him to dangle by one leg as they swept low over the rooftops. Angelchrist felt anger welling up inside of him.

Above, a thickening cloud of Squall had begun to form in the sky behind them. 'There are scores of them, Doctor. More. They're giving chase.'

'Oh,' said the Doctor, reaching up and triggering something beneath the brim of his hat, 'that's just the beginning, professor.'

Chapter
13

London, 17 October 1910

Rory couldn't believe the sheer speed that the Doctor was managing to wring from the ancient, open-topped vehicle. Appearances, it seemed, could be deceptive. It looked more like a black, motorised carriage than a car – which, he supposed, it was – but whatever the Doctor was doing, it was charging along at a fair lick.

He supposed the vehicle itself was probably relatively new, even though the technology was now considerably outmoded. At least, it would be a hundred years from now. He wondered if the Doctor had used his sonic screwdriver to tinker with it earlier, making a few casual adjustments to improve its performance. It wouldn't have surprised him: the thing was charging along nearly as fast as his Mini.

Rory himself was currently kneeling on the back seat beside Amy, clutching the wooden Neanderthal's club he'd taken from the professor's laboratory and warily eyeing the skies.

Behind them, the vast cloud of Squall was like an oil slick across the sky. To Rory it looked as if the heavens themselves had opened to spew forth multitudes of the parasites, pouring them out into the sky. They were everywhere he looked, thousands of them, streaming toward the vehicle – and more specifically the Doctor – on their fleshy wings. Even the sunlight itself had taken on a hazy, grainy quality, as if the sky had suddenly become overcast with dark, pregnant rainclouds.

The Doctor, it seemed, was barely in control of the vehicle. It slewed crazily from side to side, sliding around corners, tipping up on two wheels as he tried to manoeuvre it around the winding streets. The engine was protesting loudly at this mistreatment, and Rory feared that at some point soon it was going to give up on them. He hoped they'd be able to make it to their destination before it came to that.

Maddeningly, the Doctor himself seemed to be enjoying the whole experience, a broad grin on his face, one hand clutching the top hat to his head to ensure that it wasn't swept away in a sudden gust.

'Hold her steady,' Rory called to the Doctor, as an errant Squall lurched out at them from its perch atop a lamppost, baring its fangs and hissing as it swept low as if aiming to snatch Rory from his seat.

He scrambled to his feet, balancing precariously on the seat and swinging the Neanderthal's club for all that he was worth. It connected with a resounding *thud*, striking the creature in the chest and causing it to buckle over, dropping to the ground and spinning away as the car shot off into the distance.

Rory dropped back to his knees, his heart pounding.

'Oooh, caveman. Who'd have thought it?' said Amy, pouting provocatively. 'Rory Williams going all primal and protective on me.'

Rory felt his cheeks flush with embarrassment. He thought about trying for a witty response, but his brain failed to provide him with anything suitably roguish.

Seconds later he was grabbing her by the head, shoving her down into the seat to avoid the sweeping talons of another Squall.

The Doctor, realising they were in trouble, spun the wheel and sent the vehicle careening down a narrow alleyway. Rory had to lean in to avoid bashing his head on the wall as the side of the car scraped loudly against the brickwork, sparks flying. The side lamp went pinging off into the air, and the Squall was left rolling in the gutter far behind them.

'Sorry, professor!' said the Doctor, cringing, as they juddered along the cobbled road. A flurry of Squall shot through the narrow passageway in pursuit, chittering and screeching angrily.

They burst out of the alleyway a moment later,

right into the path of oncoming traffic. The car bucked and swerved, and there was a scream from somewhere to Rory's left. He looked round to see a young woman with a pram, diving out of the way of the onrushing car.

'Whhhooooaaaaa!' called the Doctor, steering hard to the right and bouncing them up over the curb and onto the pavement. Pedestrians scattered every which way with a flurry of curses and protestations.

'Sorry!' called the Doctor at the top of his lungs, as he bounced the vehicle back down onto the road. People continued to scatter, screaming in sheer horror, and for the slightest of moments Rory was left wondering why the Doctor's driving – as terrible as it was – had spooked them quite so dramatically. Until the dark shadow of the Squall spread once more overhead, that was, and he looked up at the awe-inspiring sight above.

'Take the wheel!' he heard the Doctor shout to Angelchrist, and turned to see the him grappling with a Squall that had managed to drop down onto the bonnet and reach over, wrapping one hand around the Doctor's throat.

The Doctor, however, wasn't standing for any nonsense and pulled the creature over the windscreen and into the car, where it squirmed and fought, causing Angelchrist all manner of difficulties as he leaned over and tried desperately to operate the controls of the vehicle.

Amy reached over, grabbed for the professor's

mace – which he'd abandoned on his seat while he grappled with the steering wheel – and struck the Squall squarely and efficiently on the head. A second later it stopped writhing, out cold, and the Doctor lifted it and tossed it over the side of the car. It landed heavily on a fruit stand by the side of the road, scattering crates full of oranges and lemons across the pavement. Rory watched them roll across the cobbles like colourful marbles.

Checking his hat was still in place, the Doctor gave Amy an impish grin, and then dropped back into his seat and reclaimed the controls from Angelchrist.

The sky now was full of the creatures, forming a vast, intricate canopy across the city, and Rory could almost have believed they were actually trapped inside a huge, fleshy dome. All he could see across the rooftops were legions of Squall, stretching into the distance as far as the eye could see.

'I can't believe there're so many of them,' he said, to no one in particular. He leaned forward, calling to the Doctor. 'Do you know what you're doing, Doctor?'

'I hope so, Rory!' came the disconcerting reply.

'I've got to stop doing that,' said Rory, cursing himself.

'What?' asked Amy.

'Asking him questions when I really don't want to know the answers.'

Amy laughed, her eyes sparkling. He realised then that she, too, was enjoying herself. Despite the threat, despite whatever terrible things might happen to them and however scared she was, Amy was relishing every single moment.

'I love you, Amy Pond,' he said, but her reply was lost to the wind.

Rory hefted his club, returned to his position on the back seat and continued to survey the sky. In the front, Angelchrist was doing the same.

'We're nearly there,' said Amy a moment later, raising her voice over the noise of the engine. 'I recognise this street. This is close to where we first arrived.'

'I'm not going to have time to stop and open the gate,' said the Doctor, twisting in his seat and shouting to make sure he could be heard over the noise. 'The moment we slow down the Squall will be all over us, and I need to get inside that time ship.' He paused for a moment as he swung the car haphazardly around a horse and cart, startling the animal and causing it to whinny and bolt. 'I want you to brace yourselves,' he continued, 'and when we finally come to rest I want you out of the car and taking cover. You got that?'

Rory glanced at Amy and they both nodded their assurances to the Doctor.

'You too, professor.'

'Very well,' said Angelchrist, 'I'm ready.'

Glancing back at the road, the Doctor peered over the top of the shattered windscreen and then forced the vehicle into a hard right turn, keeping his foot flat on the accelerator and causing the back end to skid out wildly into the street. One front wheel bounced over a curb, jolting them painfully in their seats, and then they were charging along another narrow alleyway, the sides of the car rebounding from the walls. Rory felt like his stomach was somewhere in his chest.

'Get ready!' the Doctor called. 'Here it comes…'

'Oh no,' said Rory in dismay. 'He's not…'

'He is,' said Amy, grinning. 'He's going to drive straight through…'

Rory covered his head and braced himself as the Doctor turned the wheel sharply, sending them careening toward the back gate of the terraced house where the time ship had originally deposited them in London.

'We're going to die!' called Rory. 'We're all going to die!'

'Geronimooooooo!'

There was an enormous *crunch* as the wooden gate exploded in a shower of splinters and the car burst through, tumbling down the stone steps in a riot of tortured metal. Seconds later it slewed to a stop, a hair's breadth from the wall, half on its side, the front passenger wheel buried amongst a patch of begonias.

The Doctor was up and out of his seat in a matter of moments, charging toward the abandoned time ship and diving in through the open hatch.

'Come on!' said Rory, grabbing Amy by the arm and dragging her free of the wrecked vehicle. He looked at her questioningly and she nodded, looking a little dazed.

'Are you hurt, professor?' he called to Angelchrist as he dropped over the side of the wreck.

'No,' replied Angelchrist. 'No, I'm all right,' he said, levering himself out of the crumpled nose of his car.

Overhead, the swarm was already descending, spinning out of the sky in a great funnel, a torrent of deadly Squall. It was like being trapped in a perpetual twilight, like being outside at the moment of a solar eclipse, a sudden darkness descending upon the world.

'DOCTOR!' The voice of the Squall boomed like a detonating thunderclap high above the city as a thousand or more of the drones spoke in unison. 'WE HUNGER.'

'Get behind the car, now!' shouted Rory, diving over into the flowerbed and crouching down behind the vehicle. One of the rear wheels was still spinning slowly and he could smell oil seeping out of the cracked engine housing.

Amy and Angelchrist hunkered down beside him, watching in horror as the Squall rained down upon the time ship. They forced their way in through the open hatchway, filling the sky in a blizzard of talons and wings. The noise was horrendous, a cacophony of screeching and wailing, and Rory, Amy and Angelchrist covered their ears, trying to blot it out.

'Oh, Doctor…' said Amy.

Rory didn't know what to do, what to say to her,

so instead he simply watched, waiting for something to happen, waiting for the Doctor to do his work.

'Oh, no!' Angelchrist cried a second later, as the limp form of the Doctor appeared in the hatchway, clutched in the claws of one of the Squall. He was hanging slackly, like one of Amy's Raggedy Doctor dolls from her childhood. The top hat had fallen from his head, and his jacket had been shredded on his back.

'Doctor!' called Amy, climbing to her feet. 'Doctor!' She started forward but Rory caught her around the waist, dragging her back behind the relative safety of the ruined car. She drummed her fists against him in frustrated rage.

Angelchrist, however, was on his feet too. 'Get back!' he called to the Squall, charging forward and swinging the mace in a series of wide arcs, sending Squall reeling with every blow. He leapt forward, grabbing for the Doctor, just as the Squall encircled him, blotting them both entirely from view.

There was a sound like rending metal, like the universe itself was screaming in abject pain.

Everything went white.

Chapter
14

London, 17 October 1910

Rory couldn't see a thing.

He had the notion he was lying on a bed of damp soil, his arms splayed. He scrunched up his fingers and felt them sink into the moist earth. His head was swimming.

He sat up, rubbing his eyes, and immediately wished he hadn't. He spent a moment picking at the mulch he had inadvertently spread over his face. He felt disorientated, and he had the sense that something momentous had happened, but for the life of him he couldn't quite remember what it was.

Peeling open his eyes he saw the overturned wreckage of Professor Angelchrist's car and the gaping hole in the wall of the house, and everything came back to him in a flood.

Rory got to his feet, searching for Amy. She was

sitting slouched against the wall and rubbing the back of her head. She looked up at him with bleary eyes as he approached.

'What happened to your face?' she said.

'Oh, you know. The explosion...' he said, as if that would explain the streaks of mud around his eyes. He watched her eyes widen in horror as the realisation of what had happened suddenly dawned on her.

She scrambled to her feet, looking around frantically for the Doctor and Angelchrist. 'They're gone,' she said, her voice breaking. 'They're gone!'

Rory watched as she picked her way out from behind the wreck of the professor's car, her boots leaving deep impressions in the muddy loam. He followed behind her, feeling numb.

He glanced up at the sky. There was no sign of the Squall. He could see nothing but a smattering of wispy clouds in an otherwise blue sky, a flock of starlings turning wheels in the distance. Everything seemed inordinately quiet after the chaos of a few minutes earlier.

Was that it? Was it over?

Rory approached the hole in the wall where the nose of the time ship had been embedded. Through it he could see into the kitchen. The dresser was stacked high with ornamental plates, the table still dressed for dinner. It was like a moment frozen in time, as if someone had been suddenly interrupted and had never made it back to what they were doing.

He ran his hand around the edges of the hole. They were glassy and smooth, as though someone had used a power tool to cut a perfect circle in the brickwork and then buffed the rough edges until they were polished and slick. Other than that, a few broken flagstones and a deep furrow in the flowerbed were all that was left to show where the wreckage of the time ship had been.

The Doctor and Angelchrist were nowhere to be seen.

'Where is he?' said Amy, her voice edged with panic. 'Where's the Doctor?'

Rory took a deep breath. He'd been dreading a conversation like this. He'd feared that one day, travelling with the Doctor, he might find himself in this position. And now it was here. 'I think he's gone, Amy.'

'Well I can see that,' she snapped. 'But where?' She was still searching the garden frantically, as if she expected him to just pop up at any moment.

'No. No, Amy,' he said, his voice level. 'I mean *gone*.'

She turned to him, her eyes pleading. 'Don't say it. Don't say it, Rory.'

'I think he and the professor must have been caught up in the implosion,' he said, his voice barely above a whisper. 'They went with the ship, sucked through the rift.'

A single tear rolled down Amy's cheek, and he could see that she was holding back a flood. He thought that his heart might break at any moment.

He went to her, snatching her up in his arms, and she squeezed him tightly, her head resting on his shoulder. 'It'll be OK,' he said. 'We'll be OK.'

They stood for a moment, holding each other in silence, both of them numbed by the gravity of what had occurred.

There were worse places to be stuck, Rory supposed, than London in 1910. The two of them could make a life here. They could settle down, start a family. They could—

Rory felt a gust of wind stir his hair, causing him to blink, and he turned to see fallen leaves dancing around their feet as if stirred by an invisible stick. 'Hold on,' he said. 'Hold on!'

The air was rent by the sudden, wheezing roar of the TARDIS's engines, as the blue box folded into reality with a resounding clang a few metres from where they were standing. Amy swiftly disentangled herself from Rory's embrace, pushing him back.

'Doctor?' she called, and he could hear the hope in her voice. 'Doctor?'

There was no reply.

She ran to the TARDIS, throwing open the doors. 'Rory! Quickly!' she called, disappearing inside. Rory rushed after her.

The scene in the TARDIS was one of devastation. The floor was covered with the scattered remnants of the time ship. Bits of it were strewn everywhere, and Rory had to fight his way in through the door, stepping over bits of jagged metal and trailing wires. A curved piece of the ship's hull, like the shattered ribcage of a huge, metallic beast, lay resting against the central dais. Smaller fragments of metal plating, loops of cable and broken circuit boards formed a sea of ruination.

It was as if the fragmented components of the time ship had been scooped somehow from within the heart of the implosion.

At the centre of this mess, the Doctor and Angelchrist lay still and unconscious.

Amy ran to the Doctor's side and Rory went to Angelchrist, dropping to his knees and checking for a pulse. 'He's still breathing,' he called to Amy.

Amy was cradling the Doctor's head in her lap. He looked pale and drawn. His hair was mussed and dark streaks covered his cheeks where the Squall had caused him to weep blood. His jacket was torn, his shirt had been pulled open and his bow tie was askew.

'Is he alive?' asked Rory, urgently. He wasn't sure he wanted to hear the answer.

'I think so,' said Amy. 'I think so.' She brushed the Doctor's hair back from his face. 'Doctor? It's time to wake up now, Doctor,' she said, in her 'I'm not putting up with this any longer' voice.

Rory made sure Angelchrist was stable and then picked his way through the wreckage towards her. He looked down at the Doctor. He looked peaceful, almost serene, lying there in Amy's arms. 'Doctor?' said Rory, softly.

The Doctor's eyes blinked open with a sudden start. He glanced up at Rory in surprise, and then sat bolt upright, almost sending Amy flying. He looked around, as if startled to find himself there, in the TARDIS, surrounded by a sea of debris.

'Right. Yes. TARDIS,' he said, although the expression on his face betrayed his disorientation. He looked at Amy and then Rory in turn. 'Right. Let's check. Legs, hands, head, fingers, ears. Excellent! You're both still in one piece.' He frowned. 'Although, *really*, Amy. You're covered in mud. Just look at the state of your knees.'

Amy rolled her eyes and made a sound that was halfway between a sob and a laugh. She threw her arms around the Doctor's neck and planted a huge kiss on his cheek.

Rory looked on with a crooked smile, as the Doctor patted her awkwardly on the back. 'OK. Right. Things to do,' he said, getting to his feet. 'Have the Squall gone?'

Rory gave a nod of confirmation. 'Yes. Gone. All of them. It worked.'

'It worked!' echoed the Doctor, as if surprised by the very idea of it. He gave Rory an affectionate punch on the arm. 'Excellent. Good job. Best just check the scanner to make sure that rift has closed. Then we can think about tidying up this mess.' He stopped as he glanced round at the wreckage, his eyes settling on the prone form of Professor Angelchrist, still lying atop a bundle of severed cables. 'Oh dear,' he said.

The Doctor dashed over to the old man, lifting his head. 'Help me get him outside.'

Rory helped the Doctor carry the professor out into the late morning sun, laying him softly on the flowerbed beside his car.

'Give him a moment,' said the Doctor. 'He'll be fine. The fresh air will do him the world of good.' He stood back, dusting himself down as if the action would make any difference at all to the state of his shredded jacket.

'So, Doctor... How did you...?' said Amy, glancing over at the TARDIS.

'Oh,' said the Doctor. 'Yes, that. Simple, really. I programmed the TARDIS to home in on my psychic signal at the moment of the implosion, scooping me out before I was dragged through the rift along with the Squall.'

'But how?' said Rory? 'I thought you said you couldn't risk the TARDIS getting caught up in the implosion.'

The Doctor gave him a sly grin. 'The hive sees all. The hive knows all,' he parroted. 'The hive mind was listening, Rory. It was in the TARDIS's telepathic circuits. If it knew what I was going to do it really would have tried to interfere with the old girl's dematerialisation.'

'So you were bluffing?' said Rory.

The Doctor grinned. 'Bluffing? Me?' He looked down at the sound of Angelchrist stirring amongst the begonias. 'Ah, professor. Hello!'

Angelchrist slowly opened his eyes and looked up at the three of them standing over him. He seemed startled. 'Doctor?' he said, perplexed. 'You're alive.'

'Yes,' said the Doctor, laughing, 'and so are you.'

Angelchrist pulled himself into a sitting position and patted himself on the chest, as if he didn't really believe what the Doctor was telling him. 'Yes, it rather appears I am,' he said brightly, dusting himself off.

Rory reached down and helped the professor to his feet.

'Is it over?' said Angelchrist, staring at the enormous hole in the side of the building. 'Did I miss it? Have they gone?'

'Yes, it's over,' said the Doctor. He put his hand on the wheel of the partially overturned vehicle beside him, patting it ruefully. 'Although I'm afraid it looks as if you might be needing a lift home.'

Angelchrist laughed. 'Actually, Doctor, I was wondering if, before I head back to that dreary old house of mine, you might humour an old man with a favour?'

The Doctor's face split into a wide Cheshire grin. 'Name it,' he said.

'Just once, I'd dearly love to see the stars. See them as they were meant to be seen, from up there,' he glanced up at the sky. 'Do you think that might be possible?'

'I think, professor, that anything's possible, if you put your mind to it. Anything at all.' He put his arm around Angelchrist's shoulders and led him in the direction of the TARDIS. 'But first there's the matter of all this junk to get rid of. I know just the place. Only a short hop away…' The Doctor's voice trailed off as they disappeared inside the TARDIS.

Amy, laughing, skipped into the ship behind them.

Rory stood for a moment in the garden, glancing from the wreckage of the professor's car to the hole in the side of the house. He shook his head in disbelief. Even now, after all the time he'd spent with the Doctor, he still had to pinch himself from time to time to remind himself it was real. Every day with the Doctor was another madcap adventure, a day filled with hair-raising escapades or glimpses into the distant future, a day filled with aliens made of wool, with vampire creatures from the stars or exploding nuclear bombs.

He, Rory Williams, the plain old nurse from Leadworth, had not only got the girl, but she'd taken him on the trip of a lifetime, too. And he loved every minute of it.

Grinning, he went to join the others.

Chapter
15

Angelchrist stood by the open doors of the TARDIS, clutching the wooden frame and peering out in wonder at the magnificent vista beyond. To him, it was as if he were seeing the universe properly for the first time, the sheer scale of it, the beauty. He'd always wondered what it would be like, but even in his wildest imaginings he had never come close to the truth. So much colour, so much vibrancy, so much life. He could barely take it all in. He gazed out into the depths of space, at the millions of shimmering stars, prickling the canopy of black like diamonds strewn across a blanket; at distant, twirling nebulae; at the stately dance of a gas giant slowly revolving around its sun.

'All those worlds… it's dazzling,' he said.

Things for Angelchrist would never be the same

again, not after this. All those petty concerns, all those fears about the future, about being left behind on the shelf, they amounted to nothing when held up against the backdrop of the universe. The Doctor had shown him wonders. The Doctor had changed his life.

He felt tears welling in his eyes, but fought them back. Now wasn't the time. Tears would only spoil the view.

'All those years, Doctor. All those years working for the British government, defending the realm against alien incursions. It seemed so important, so big. But I could never have imagined the sheer scale of this. The immensity of it.'

The Doctor, leaning on the opposite side of the doorframe in his shirtsleeves and braces, smiled. 'Yes. It's a wonderful place, this universe of ours. For all the monsters and the madness, all the horrors and the wars, there are moments like this. The universe finds a balance.'

Angelchrist was almost lost for words. 'Thank you, Doctor,' he said. 'Thank you. You've saved an old man from himself.'

'No, not at all, professor. You did that entirely on your own.'

Angelchrist turned back to the view.

'Arven would have loved it up here,' said Rory a moment later, his voice tinged with sadness. Angelchrist felt a momentary twinge of loss for the artificial man.

'Arven!' said the Doctor. 'Of course!' He ran over

to the console, punching in coordinates. 'We have a date to keep!'

'A date?' said Amy. 'What kind of date?'

'A date in the twenty-eighth century,' said the Doctor, moving around the console, his fingers dancing over the controls. He clicked his fingers and the TARDIS doors snapped shut. 'Sorry, professor,' he said. 'Places to go, people to see.'

Angelchrist stepped away from the doors, moving to stand by a guard rail. He was still feeling overwhelmed by the momentousness of the occasion.

The central column burred and sighed, and a few moments later the engines shuddered with a pneumatic wheeze and the TARDIS came to a stop.

'Now, listen,' said the Doctor, wagging his finger at Amy. 'This is very important. No wandering off. Stick together. It's absolutely *essential* that we're not seen.'

Amy put one hand on her hip, and frowned. 'What are you up to, Doctor?'

'Fulfilling a promise to a friend,' he said, beckoning them toward the door. 'Prepare yourself, professor,' he said, as they stepped out into the bright sunshine.

They were standing on the bank of a river, looking out over the immense sprawl of a city. Huge glass domes nestled amongst ancient ornamental buildings. Towers of metal and glass shimmered in the reflected sunlight, scraping the underside of the clouds. The river buzzed with life; strange little boats that shot up and down the waterways leaving trails of white spray in their wake; tiny skiffs and enormous, sleek-looking tankers; yachts and ferries. Angelchrist gaped. 'Is this... Is this *London*?'

The Doctor smiled but didn't say anything.

'I've never seen anything like it,' Angelchrist continued.

'This spot seems very familiar,' said Amy, leaning on the Doctor as she peered out over the river.

'Hang on a minute,' said Rory. 'Look, that's us!'

'Shhh!' chided the Doctor. 'Keep your voice down, Rory! I told you, it's vital that they don't notice us.' He put one hand on top of Rory's head and the other on top of Amy's, and pushed them both down until they were all crouching behind a railing, out of sight.

Angelchrist, bewildered, watched the Doctor, Amy and Rory – alternate versions of the Doctor, Amy, and Rory – strolling merrily along the embankment no more than fifty metres away. They were heading toward a group of people dressed in what he imagined to be diving costumes. They appeared to be lifting something out of the river.

'This looks *spectacularly* interesting,' said the other Doctor, and the Doctor beside Angelchrist cringed in embarrassment.

'Do I sound like that?' he asked Amy.

'Yes,' she said, laughing heartily. 'That's *exactly* how you sound.'

'I *thought* I was being watched,' said Rory. 'I knew it!'

'What is this, Doctor?' asked Angelchrist, his voice strained. 'Who are those people?'

'That's us,' said the Doctor. 'Us four days ago, when we first arrived in London.'

'But how can that be? How can you be in the same place twice over?'

'And I thought we weren't supposed to cross our own timelines?' added Amy mischievously.

'Yes, well, questions, questions,' said the Doctor with a wave of his hand. 'Always questions.'

Rory was leaning out through the railing, watching the proceedings on the embankment with interest. 'We never did work out what brought us here in the first place,' he said, peering down at his doppelgänger. 'What caused the TARDIS to bring us here, to this exact time and place.'

'Oh no, Rory. That was me,' said the Doctor.

'What do you mean, it was you?'

'Back at the professor's house. Before Arven was taken by the Squall, before he dismantled the barricade, I made a few... modifications. Gave him a little tweak. I fiddled with his energy signature so that the TARDIS would fix on him when he was pulled out of the water.'

'Like a distress beacon,' said Amy.

'Precisely!' said the Doctor.

'But that doesn't make sense,' said Rory. 'Cause and effect. The TARDIS heard his distress call before you ever met him.'

'Pah! Cause and effect?' said the Doctor, grinning. 'Noodley soup, remember?' He wiggled his fingers as if to illustrate his point.

'You did something else, too, didn't you?' said Amy. 'To Arven, I mean. That's why we're here.'

The Doctor gave her a coy smile. 'Ah, look, we're leaving,' he said, pointing to the group of people down by the river. The other Amy had looped her arm through the other Rory's and was dragging him off along the embankment.

'I'm pleased to report that the city conservation board are satisfied with everything you're doing here. Please do carry on,' called the other Doctor to a smartly dressed woman, who watched him, perplexed, as he hared off towards his waiting TARDIS.

'Right,' said the Doctor, emerging from behind the railing. 'Come on then.' He led the four of them down towards the water's edge. Angelchrist tried to drink it all in, soaking up the sights of this strange, futuristic version of his city as he ambled along behind the others.

'Hello!' said the Doctor amiably, as they approached the woman in the blue suit. 'Patricia, isn't it?' She turned to look at the Doctor, a look of confusion on her face. 'Didn't you just go *that* way?'

'Um, yes. Sort of,' said the Doctor. 'Long story.' He fiddled nervously with his bow tie. 'Anyway, enough of that.'

'You look different,' said the woman, ignoring him. 'Have you changed your jacket?'

The Doctor gave her a charming grin. 'Yes, well.

A change is as good as a rest, as they say. All very jolly. Nice to see you again and all that. Thing is, there's something I forgot. With the AI. Terribly important.'

'Oh yes?' said the woman, leadingly. 'For the city conservation board, is it?'

'Exactly that,' said the Doctor, clicking his fingers.

'Be my guest,' she said with a sigh, stepping to one side to let the Doctor pass.

The group of men behind the woman were carrying something on a pallet. Angelchrist assumed it was the thing he'd seen them dredging the river for just a few moments earlier.

'Sorry, chaps,' said the Doctor. 'I won't be a moment.' He approached the pallet, and Angelchrist watched him with interest. The men lowered the pallet to the ground with a few mumbled words of protest, which the Doctor studiously ignored.

The thing on the pallet was a great hunk of rusting metal, the remains of some complex machine that had clearly been dumped in the water some years earlier. Angelchrist couldn't make head or tail of what it might originally have been. Neither had he any idea what the Doctor might want with it.

'Oh, Arven,' said Amy, looking sadly at the object.

'Arven?' exclaimed Angelchrist loudly, and the five men who'd been carrying the pallet all looked up to see what the fuss was about. Angelchrist ignored them. He looked again, realising that the object on the pallet was actually the skeletal remains of an artificial man. It was badly decomposed, pitted and scarred, and most of its rubbery flesh had long since been stripped away. It was missing an arm and part of its left leg.

'Arven,' he said, in disbelief. 'It really is, isn't it? Is that what becomes of him? What became of him after the Squall?'

Rory nodded. 'I'm afraid so, professor. They ditched him in the river over a thousand years ago.'

'Ah, but...' said the Doctor, and Angelchrist looked over to see him using his sonic screwdriver to pop open a small panel in the side of Arven's chest. 'Those minor modifications I was talking about...' He stuck his fingers into the hole, grimacing as he fished out a small metal cylinder about the size of Angelchrist's thumb. It was attached to the internal workings of the AI by three small wires, which the Doctor yanked free, before holding the object up to the light and squinting at it with one eye. 'Might just mean that this little object here contains everything we need to bring him back,' finished the Doctor, glancing at Rory with a triumphant expression on his face.

'What is it?' said Amy.

'Backup memory,' said the Doctor. 'Ancillary storage. I made a copy of Arven's consciousness, locking it inside this tiny memory cell. It has its own residual power. With any luck it'll have survived a thousand years in the River Thames, too.'

'You mean you can bring him back?' said Rory hopefully.

'I mean exactly that,' replied the Doctor. 'A quick trip to Villiers Artificial Life laboratory in Battersea, and we should be able to upload the contents of this little beauty into a spanking new body.' He glanced down at the rusted remains on the pallet. 'The long way home,' he said, quietly.

'You're a remarkable man, Doctor,' said Angelchrist warmly.

'Oh, I don't know about that,' said the Doctor, grinning, 'but I'd be a pretty useless magician if I didn't have at least a few tricks up my sleeve.' He pocketed the memory cell and put a hand on Angelchrist's arm, leading him away toward the TARDIS. 'Now. I think, professor, it's about time we were getting you home.'

Angelchrist sighed. Yes. Home. For once, the idea filled him with a sense of wellbeing rather than abject dread. 'You're right, Doctor. And besides, I rather imagine I'll have some tidying up to do.'

'What about Arven?' said Rory, falling into step as they drifted away from the remains of the AI, leaving a baffled Patricia Young staring after them, shaking her head.

'Oh, he's waited a thousand years, Rory,' said the Doctor. 'A few more hours won't make any difference to him now.'

Nodding, Rory dropped back, waiting for Amy to catch up. Angelchrist watched them as the Doctor fished for the TARDIS key in his jacket pocket. They were quite a couple, accompanying the Doctor on all of his wild adventures. He didn't think he'd have the pace to keep up with them for very long, anyway. Not with all that running.

He saw Rory take Amy's hand. 'Are you ready?' he said.

'I love you, Rory Williams,' came her reply. She had a playful gleam in her eyes.

'I'll take that as a yes,' said Rory, and together, with Angelchrist, they followed the Doctor into his magical blue box.

Epilogue

London, 23 October 1921

Angelchrist drained the last dregs of his tea and reached over, placing the empty teacup on the table beside his upturned copy of *The War of the Worlds*. He'd enjoyed a relaxing, lazy afternoon, snoozing in his chair and dipping in and out of Mr Wells's novel. It had always been a favourite of his, ever since he'd seen the author speak about it at a bookshop on Charing Cross Road over twenty years earlier. The events it described were in no way a reflection of Angelchrist's own experiences of alien incursions, but it *was*, he supposed, a work of fiction, intended to provoke the mind and entertain the spirit. In that respect, it was an utter triumph. Absently, he wondered what the Doctor would have made of it.

It had been some time since he'd thought about the strange man and his cabinet of tricks. Over a decade had passed since they'd met by the river on Cheyne Walk, since the Squall had attacked the city and practically pulled Angelchrist's house to pieces. Much had happened in the intervening years. War had come and gone, for a start. The world was changing all around him.

The years had slid by and Angelchrist had filled them well, he thought, involving himself in the machinations of the secret service or aiding Scotland Yard when they needed his particular brand of specialist assistance. He'd rebuilt his laboratory and had continued to indulge his passion for invention.

He'd heard occasional reports of the Doctor, too, over the years, some of them stretching back years into the past. Just before the outbreak of the Great War he'd spent some time digging around in the government archives, finding mention of the Doctor in a plethora of obscure reports; a sly reference in a footnote or a scrawled note in a margin. It appeared as if the Doctor had made walk-on appearances at many of the crucial events of the last hundred years.

Slowly, Angelchrist had been able to build a picture. It seemed the Doctor sometimes wore different faces and travelled with different companions. The descriptions he had found were unclear on this point. Sometimes the Doctor was described as a tall, thin man with long hair and a frock coat. Other times he was all teeth and curls, a long woollen scarf draped around his shoulders. Other times still he wore a black leather jacket and spoke with a Northern accent, or a pantomime coat of many colours. Always, however, he travelled in a remarkable blue box, appearing as if out of the ether to aid in whatever crisis was ongoing.

Then, of course, there was *his* Doctor. Angelchrist's Doctor, the man in the tweed jacket, bow tie and braces, the awkward one who stumbled about the place, tripping over himself as he set about saving the world. Angelchrist had never filed *that* report. He wondered how many other people had done the same, how many times the Doctor had stepped in to save the Earth and then slipped away again in the dead of night, his passing unrecorded.

Sighing, Angelchrist reached for his book. Another chapter, he thought, before he'd head to the kitchen and make a start on his supper.

Just as he was settling back into his chair, there was a loud rap on the door. Angelchrist groaned in frustration. No. They could ruddy well go away. He was tired, and he wanted to enjoy his book. Didn't they know what time it was? He turned to the correct page and scanned the first line.

There was another knock, this time more insistent.

Cursing, Angelchrist slammed his book down on the arm of his chair and pulled himself up out of his seat. 'Yes, yes!' he called, resignedly. 'I'm coming.'

In the hallway he could hear voices from outside, talking urgently in low tones. He hoped they weren't going to attempt to sell him something.

He crossed to the door, slid the chain off the

latch and pulled it open. He glared out with what he hoped was a withering stare. His eyes widened in shock, however, when he saw three familiar faces beaming back at him.

'Hello, professor!' said the Doctor, grabbing Angelchrist's hand and pumping it furiously. 'Sorry to be a pest. Slight issue. You see, I think I left something here the other week. It's a wrench. Sonic one. Got a problem with a Sarkovian warlord and that wrench could be the key to...' He trailed off, a look of concern on his face. 'Oh. Have I got it wrong again? Haven't we met yet?' He stepped back, looking Angelchrist up and down appraisingly.

Angelchrist stared at the Doctor, unsure what to say. He looked exactly the same as he had all those years ago.

Angelchrist's mouth moved but no sound came out. The Doctor raised his eyebrows in encouragement, urging him on. 'But Doctor... it's been ten years!' he finally managed to blurt out a moment later.

'Ten years!' said the Doctor. 'Oh dear...'

'He's *always* doing that,' said Amy knowingly.

'Not looking good for the wrench, then,' said the Doctor with a sigh. 'Still, could be worse. It could be the entire galactic arm under threat, rather than just one little part of it. Besides, there's another reason we're here. I hope you don't mind – I brought a friend.' The Doctor beckoned off to his left, and a tall figure stepped into view from around the corner. The man was at least two metres tall, with pale flesh and a smooth, bald head. He was wrapped in a long winter coat. Angelchrist felt his spirits lift as he recognised the familiar, placid face.

'Arven!' said Angelchrist in delight.

'Hello, professor,' said the artificial man. He stepped closer, and Angelchrist saw that his face – once so damaged – was now perfect and unblemished. 'It's good to see you again after all this time.'

'So you were true to your word, Doctor. You found him a new body. I never doubted you would.'

The Doctor beamed. 'Thing is, professor, Arven's got nowhere to go. His former employer is dead, and artificial people won't be granted their liberty for at least another century or two after Arven's time. So we got to thinking...' The Doctor glanced at Amy and Rory, and then at Angelchrist once again, '... about you, rattling around in this big house of yours, and how you could probably do with some company.' He paused for a moment, grinning. 'So, what do you say?'

'Well, I...' Angelchrist stammered, momentarily taken aback. But then he allowed a broad grin to break out on his face. 'I'd be honoured,' he said, looking over at Arven, who was smiling in the watery evening sunlight.

'Good. That's settled, then.' The Doctor patted Arven on the shoulder. 'Oooh,' he said suddenly, leaning forward and peering into the house. 'Is that a fresh pot of tea I can smell?'

Angelchrist, shaking his head in disbelief, stepped

back into the hallway, ushering them inside. 'Yes, it is, Doctor. I suppose you'd better come in. Only, try not to wreck the place this time. It took me years to put it right again.'

'Excellent!' said the Doctor, hopping up onto the step. 'You grab the teacups and I'll fill you in about those pesky Sarkovians.'

Angelchrist watched as the Doctor, Amy, Rory and Arven filed in from the cold, tramping through noisily into the drawing room. He stood for a moment in the doorway, glancing up at the twinkling stars, and laughed.

Acknowledgements

With special thanks to Kat and Justin for connecting the dots. Also to Paul, Stuart, Mark and Cav for their continued friendship and support.

Apollo 23

by Justin Richards

£6.99 ISBN 978 1 846 07200 0

An astronaut in full spacesuit appears out of thin air in a busy shopping centre. Maybe it's a publicity stunt.

A photo shows a well-dressed woman in a red coat lying dead at the edge of a crater on the dark side of the moon, beside her beloved dog 'Poochie'. Maybe it's a hoax.

But as the Doctor and Amy find out, these are just minor events in a sinister plan to take over every human being on Earth. The plot centres on a secret military base on the moon – that's where Amy and the TARDIS are.

The Doctor is back on Earth, and without the TARDIS there's no way he can get to the moon to save Amy and defeat the aliens.

Or is there? The Doctor discovers one last great secret that could save humanity: Apollo 23.

A thrilling, all-new adventure featuring the Doctor and Amy, as played by Matt Smith and Karen Gillan in the spectacular hit series from BBC Television.

DOCTOR ⊞ WHO
The Forgotten Army
by Brian Minchin

£6.99 ISBN 978 1 846 07987 0

New York – one of the greatest cities on 21st-century Earth... But what's going on in the Museum? And is that really a Woolly Mammoth rampaging down Broadway?

An ordinary day becomes a time of terror, as Ice Age creatures come back to life, and the Doctor and Amy meet a new and deadly enemy. The vicious Army of the Vykoid are armed to the teeth and determined to enslave the human race. Even though they're only three inches high.

With the Vykoid army swarming across Manhattan and sealing it from the world with a powerful alien forcefield, Amy has just 24 hours to find the Doctor and save the city. If she doesn't, the people of Manhattan will be taken to work in the doomed asteroid mines of the Vykoid home planet.

But as time starts to run out, who can she trust? And how far will she have to go to free New York from the Forgotten Army?

A thrilling, all-new adventure featuring the Doctor and Amy, as played by Matt Smith and Karen Gillan in the spectacular hit series from BBC Television.

Available now from BBC Books:

The Only Good Dalek

by Justin Richards and Mike Collins

£16.99 ISBN 978 1 846 07984 9

Station 7 is where the Earth Forces send all the equipment captured in their unceasing war against the Daleks. It's where Dalek technology is analysed and examined. It's where the Doctor and Amy have just arrived. But somehow the Daleks have found out about Station 7 – and there's something there that they want back.

With the Doctor increasingly worried about the direction the Station's research is taking, the commander of Station 7 knows he has only one possible, desperate, defence. Because the last terrible secret of Station 7 is that they don't only store captured Dalek technology. It's also a prison. And the only thing that might stop a Dalek is another Dalek...

An epic, full-colour graphic novel featuring the Doctor and Amy, as played by Matt Smith and Karen Gillan in the spectacular hit series from BBC Television.

Available now from BBC Books:

DOCTOR WHO
Dead of Winter
by James Goss

£6.99 ISBN 978 1 849 90238 0

In Dr Bloom's clinic at a remote spot on the Italian coast, at the end of the eighteenth century, nothing is ever quite what it seems.

Maria is a lonely little girl with no one to play with. She writes letters to her mother from the isolated resort where she is staying. She tells of the pale English aristocrats and the mysterious Russian nobles and their attentive servants. She tells of intrigue and secrets, and she tells of strange faceless figures that rise from the sea. She writes about the enigmatic Mrs Pond who arrives with her husband and her physician, and who will change everything.

What she doesn't tell her mother is the truth that everyone knows and no one says – that the only people who come here do so to die…

A thrilling, all-new adventure featuring the Doctor, Amy and Rory, as played by Matt Smith, Karen Gillan and Arthur Darvill in the spectacular hit series from BBC Television.

Available now from BBC Books:

DOCTOR ⬚ WHO
The Way through the Woods
by Una McCormack

£6.99 ISBN 978 1 849 90237 3

Two teenage girls disappear into an ancient wood, a foreboding and malevolent presence both now and in the past. The modern motorway bends to avoid it, as did the old Roman road.

In 1917 the Doctor and Amy are desperate to find out what's happened to Rory, who's vanished too.

But something is waiting for them in the woods. Something that's been there for thousands of years. Something that is now waking up.

A thrilling, all-new adventure featuring the Doctor, Amy and Rory, as played by Matt Smith, Karen Gillan and Arthur Darvill in the spectacular hit series from BBC Television.

DOCTOR ⬛ WHO
Hunter's Moon
by Paul Finch

£6.99 ISBN 978 1 849 90236 6

Welcome to Leisure Platform 9 – a place where gamblers and villains rub shoulders with socialites and celebrities. Don't cheat at the games tables, and be careful who you beat. The prize for winning the wrong game is to take part in another, as Rory is about to discover – and the next game could be the death of him.

When Rory is kidnapped by the brutal crime lord Xord Krauzzen, the Doctor and Amy must go undercover to infiltrate the deadly contest being played out in the ruins of Gorgoror. But how long before Krauzzen realises the Doctor isn't a vicious mercenary and discovers what Amy is up to? It's only a matter of time.

And time is the one thing Rory and the other fugitives on Gorgoror don't have. They are the hunted in a game that can only end in death, and time for everyone is running out…

A thrilling, all-new adventure featuring the Doctor, Amy and Rory, as played by Matt Smith, Karen Gillan and Arthur Darvill in the spectacular hit series from BBC Television.

Available now from BBC Books:

DOCTOR◫WHO
Touched by an Angel
by Jonathan Morris

£6.99 ISBN 978 1 849 90234 2

In 2003, Rebecca Whitaker died in a road accident. Her husband Mark is still grieving. Then he receives a battered envelope, posted eight years ago, containing a set of instructions and a letter with a simple message:

'You can save her.'

Later that night, while picking up a takeaway, Mark glances at a security monitor – to see himself, standing in the restaurant in grainy black and white. And behind him there's a stone statue of an angel. Covering its eyes, as though weeping… Except, when Mark turns, there's nothing there.

As Mark is given the chance to save Rebecca, it's up to the Doctor, Amy and Rory to save the whole world. Because this time the Weeping Angels are using history itself as a weapon…

A thrilling, all-new adventure featuring the Doctor, Amy and Rory, as played by Matt Smith, Karen Gillan and Arthur Darvill in the spectacular hit series from BBC Television.

Available now from BBC Books:

DOCTOR ⬛ WHO
Borrowed Time
by Naomi A. Alderman

£6.99 ISBN 978 1 849 90233 5

Andrew Brown never has enough time. No time to call his sister, no time to prepare for that important presentation at the bank where he works... The train's late, the lift jams, the all-important meeting's started by the time he arrives. Disaster.

If only he'd had just a little more time.

Time is the business of Mr Symington and Mr Blenkinsop. They'll lend Andrew Brown some time – at a very reasonable rate of interest. If he was in trouble before he borrowed time, things have just got a lot worse.

Detecting a problem, the Doctor, Amy and Rory go undercover at the bank. The Doctor's a respected expert, and Amy's his trusted advisor. Rory has a job in the post room. But they have to move fast to stop Symington and Blenkinsop before they cash in their investments. The Harvest is approaching.

A thrilling, all-new adventure featuring the Doctor, Amy and Rory, as played by Matt Smith, Karen Gillan and Arthur Darvill in the spectacular hit series from BBC Television.